P9-CBJ-818

A CANDLELIGHT ROMANCE

CANDLELIGHT ROMANCES

Love's Sweet Surrender

by

Arlene Hale

A CANDLELIGHT ROMANCE

Published by
Dell Publishing Co., Inc.
1 Dag Hammarskjold Plaza
New York, New York 10017

Dell ® TM 681510, Dell Publishing Co., Inc.

ISBN: 0-440-15105-8

Printed in the United States of America

Special Dell Printing—April 1981

Chapter I

Angela Wales, clad in cutoff denim shorts and a sleeveless blouse, dark hair touseled by the sea wind, was shooting film as if there were no tomorrow.

"Hold still, José. For Pete's sake, don't look so solemn! Give me that big fat grin of yours. Great! Hold it just a second. One more, José, and you can get back to whatever it was you were doing."

José's smile was as real as the sun and the sea. It beamed out from his weathered brown face like a beacon on a dark and stormy night. Angela muttered to herself, a sure sign that she was pleased with what she saw through the lens of her camera. She clicked the shutter half a dozen times.

"Okay now?" José asked.

"I could never find a better subject if I looked for a hundred years." she laughed.

José Hagar was an old, old friend, Spanish in descent, a fisherman all his life until he had retired to collect his rocking chair money as he called it. The background of his weathered cottage was perfect, too—the coil of rope lying on the porch, the nets hung up for drying (José still went fishing occasionally), the heavy coffee mug that sat on the porch railing, as battered as the old man himself. All this lent texture and dimension that Angela could find nowhere but on the island of Bella Grande, stretched out

5

lazily in the incredibly blue waters of the Gulf of Mexico, separated by a toll bridge and a causeway from the Florida shore.

"What are you going to do with all those pictures?" José demanded. "And why don't I ever see them?"

Angela laughed and pulled her sunglasses down from the top of her head, fitting them snugly on her pert nose. "Come to my show, old dear, and you'll see! You might be in for a big surprise."

"An old ugly man like me? Pooh!"

"Not ugly! Beautiful!"

"Must be better things in New York," José said.

Angela kept the bright smile on her face, but everything inside her came to a grinding halt, as if someone in a speeding car had suddenly thrown on the emergency brake, sending her into a critical spin.

"New York is great. Bella Grande is just as great. Besides, I need to come home, José. For a little while."

"Never one to let your sails lie limp for long," José said with a grin.

"I have to scat. See you, José."

Angela blew him a kiss, gathered up her camera equipment, and packed it carefully into a leather shoulderbag. Then she was off, swinging down to the edge of the water where the surf could come rushing in over her bare feet. She couldn't wait to develop the film, to see if what she thought she'd captured was really there for others to see.

"A damned perfectionist," was the way Phillip Blazer had tagged her.

"I thought that was what you wanted for the *Top Fashion Magazine*!" was her usual retort.

"For the magazine, yes, but not for everything else in our life, including me."

"I expect certain things. I won't settle for less. That's the way I am."

"You want too much," he had said darkly.

"But I'll find what I want, one way or another."

"Right now I guess that doesn't include me."

"When you can learn to leave other women alone, come

6

around and look me up. But I can't stomach it this way, Phil. Sorry."

"Arrogant as hell, aren't you? Independent, icy, and heading for a fall."

"Maybe. But if I do fall, it will be in my own way."

"Look, photographers are a dime a dozen in this business and this town."

"Meaning what?"

He had given her a long, hard look. "Shape up, honey."

She had laughed brittlely, suddenly seeing through him as if he were a pane of glass. "Be nice to the boss and keep my job, is that it?"

He had lifted his shoulders in a shrug. "It's the way it's done, you know."

"Not by me!"

She had stormed out of Phil's office and left the magazine a week later. She had saved a little money. There was Dad's comfortable and pleasant house on Bella Grande which she'd always called home, and that constant and awful itch to strike out on her own. It wasn't hard to decide to come back to Bella Grande and coast for a while.

But now as she headed down the beach swinging along with her camera snuggled over her shoulder she knew that she missed Phillip Blaze more than she had imagined she would. The hurt of parting had not been nearly as superficial as she'd led him to believe. But she never liked looking back over her shoulder. She fastened her gaze stubbornly ahead and beyond.

She began to run, giving in to an urge, enjoying the wind in her face, the wet sand under her bare toes. She kept running until she was nearly winded. By then she was near the cove where she used to come as a girl, where a little hiding place had sheltered her through more than one rocky time in her life.

It was invisible from the beach, a tiny nook tucked away into the rocks, her own personal Eden when she needed it. She'd never shared it with anyone, not even with her best friend, Kelly Ross, or with José or his darling little granddaughter, Thomasita, or Dad—no one.

She had just made herself comfortable, stretched out her

legs, and parked her camera nearby when she heard her name coming back to her on the wind. She leaned out far enough to see Michael Field standing up the beach searching vainly for sight of her. She snatched up her camera bag and left her hideaway.

"Hi!" she shouted.

He saw her then and waited, his jacket slung over his shoulder, his bright tie flapping in the salty breeze. She laughed as she came to a halt beside him. She reached up and pulled his head down to plant a fleeting kiss on his firm mouth.

"Where were you? You came out of nowhere," he said.

"Didn't you know? I'm a sea nymph."

"Among other things," he said dryly.

She took his arm. "What brings you here at this time of day? Don't tell me that the very proper Michael Field has finally decided to play hooky like everyone else at the Banner Oil offices does at one time or another."

"I swear," he said, shaking his head. "I wonder *how* I got involved with you!"

"You found me irresistible, what else?"

"Honey, I have to tell you something and I want you to keep calm. Don't go overboard and don't start giving me that look—"

She drew a deep sigh. "If you tell me you're going to duck out of our date tonight—"

"Something's brewing at the office," he said with a worried air. "I don't know what, but they're sending me to Chicago."

"What!"

"I have forty minutes to pack a bag and catch the company plane."

"Sometimes I wish I'd never heard of the Banner Oil Company!"

"I don't like it any better than you, Angela, but I have no choice. Now, are you going to come help me pack?"

"I shouldn't, but I will."

"Great." He shoved back his cuff to look at his watch. "We'd better get cracking."

"How long will you be away?" she asked as she fell in step with his long, hurried stride.

"Don't know. Ten days probably."

She stopped walking. "If you miss my show, Michael, I'll never forgive you."

"Don't say that, not even in fun."

"You're my best critic. I was planning on your being there."

"I'll do my best."

"And tonight—"

He gave her a worried look. "You'll have a good time without me, Angela. You always manage to do that—"

She punched him playfully in the ribs. "I'm going to flirt with every man at the club. I'll dance the flamenco on the table with a flower in my teeth. I'll be very seductive—"

"No chore for you," he said with a grin like the one that had first attracted her to him.

"Oh, nuts! Why does everything go wrong?"

Casa Linda, the elegant, Spanish-styled house in which she had grown up, was only a short hike away, hidden from the street by a bricked courtyard. Her father lived there alone and was pleased that she had come back to the island.

"It gets lonely in this big house. Maybe I should sell it," he had told her.

"But you won't. You love it. Always have," she had said.

"But with your mother gone now—" he had sighed. "That's why it's like heaven to have you back."

"Just don't plan on my staying. It's just a stopover—"

"I'll remember that," he had said with a grin.

"Besides, you eat, sleep, and breathe that darned oil company. You don't really need me."

"Being general manager is getting to be more of a headache every day."

When she and Michael reached the gates of the courtyard that surrounded Casa Linda, Angela snatched up her recently discarded sandals. Michael's small car was parked out in front and Angela climbed into the bucket seat, screeching at the hotness of the leather upholstery that had soaked up the scorching sunshine.

"Maybe Chicago will be cooler," Michael said hopefully.

"Bella Grande in the summertime may be hot, but there's always that sweet sea breeze. You can have Chicago and the lake—"

They roared through the streets of Bella Grande toward the hotel where Michael had a small apartment. Angela was ever aware of the clear, clean waters of the Gulf, off to the right, incredibly blue and green, touched with bouncing whitecaps, the white-winged gulls dipping and soaring, calling their squeaky songs She must have shot a hundred rolls of film of that fascinating subject and probably would shoot a hundred more before she picked up and moved on.

But suddenly she felt lonely and she reached out to put her small hand over Michael's as he gripped the steering wheel. "Don't go."

"Honey, I have to."

"We could drive over to Miami."

"Too far."

"Then a long walk in the moonlight, a very secluded beach, a midnight swim—"

"Don't tempt me!"

"We could stay and watch the sunrise—"

His eyes flickered and a flush touched his cheeks. "Lord, you make it hard, Angela. What can I say?"

"Well, at least you could say you'll miss me."

"Every second," he said.

They turned in at the hotel. Michael's apartment was masculine and orderly, typical of him. He had come from a rather staid family. She had met his parents once and found them hopelessly dull. She wondered how a man like Michael had ever looked twice at her. He categorized everything, had one way of doing things, never veered from the set pattern.

"Where do I fit into all those pigeonholes?" she wondered aloud.

10

"What did you say?" Michael asked, tugging a fresh tie into place under his collar.

"Never mind," she said with a sigh.

Michael was ready in ten minutes, his suitcase hastily packed, a bulging briefcase in his hand. She put her arms around his neck and he dropped both bags to pull her hard and close against him.

"Not even time for a proper good-bye," he murmured.

His kiss left her feeling disappointed. Then he was moving toward the door. "We have to go."

Bella Grande was a private island with most of the property owned by the oil company or their employees. It served as a depot for oil from foreign countries. The oil was stored temporarily in huge tanks before being shipped to various distribution points by rail. Angela had grown up in the shadows of those tanks.

The airfield was at the far end of the narrow strip of land, a ten-minute drive from the hotel. Michael made it in seven. The company plane was revving up, and there was barely time for a kiss before he went dashing off to board.

"Keep my car, but for goodness' sake, don't wreck it!" he shouted over his shoulder.

She watched as the plane taxied to the end of the runway and soon was hurtling down the black streak of asphalt in the white sand and lifting away, banking to turn toward Chicago.

Angela drove back home, passing the fashionable yacht club where she and Michael had intended to spend the evening. There would be action there now, people coming in from the golf course for a quick drink at the bar, and some of the Banner Oil Company wives were sure to be around, exchanging gossip and dirty jokes.

Not for me, she decided. *But maybe I'll come back tonight—*

Angela drove on, bouncing along the palm-lined streets where the trees were bent permanently by the westerly winds, the stirring green fronds as restless as she. She hated having plans changed at the last minute, although she was guilty of sometimes doing that herself. She de-

11

cided to stop by and see Kelly Ross. They were such old friends, they were more like sisters.

Kelly had settled down on the island to teach in the elementary school, and when Angela parked Michael's car in the shade, the bell rang and kids came pouring out like ants out of an ant hill.

"Hey, Angela!"

"If it isn't my bright-eyed doll, Thomasita!" Angela teased.

José's granddaughter gave her a toothless grin and came tearing toward her to lean into the car, her dark eyes flashing.

"Are you coming to my house soon?"

"I was there today. But I'll be back. Tell me, what will you do with your summer vacation?"

Thomasita shrugged. "Play on the beach, go fishing with Grandpa--just goof it up!"

Angela laughed and Thomasita was gone with a wave of her hand. shouting to some of her friends.

Angela went inside. The halls were cool. Her footsteps click-clacked as she strode quickly in her sandals.

"Okay, teacher, do you have to stay in after school?"

Angela strode into the classroom, a tall, leggy girl with a golden tan and burnished copper tones in her glossy black hair. She never walked slowly. but never looked at anything too quickly. She took in the room with a long, sweeping glance that noted all the special details, as if peering at it through the clear lens of her camera.

Kelly looked up with a quick smile, her sun-bleached blond head lifting with pleased surprise.

"This must be an emergency—to bring you here. What's up?" Kelly asked.

"Michael just left in the company plane for Chicago."

"Oh, and you're bored already."

"Want to have dinner at our house?" Angela asked.

"Can't. Date."

"You're holding out on me," Angela said. "Who is he?"

"Pete Ryan. New to the island. Not your type at all, thank God." Kelly sighed. "If Pete ever got a glimpse of you . . ."

"But you stole Bernie Williams away from me, remember?"

They began laughing, remembering an incident of their very early dating days which had nearly broken up their friendship for good.

"I have to top you at least once in a while," Kelly retorted. "What's doing with Michael?"

"Don't know. Company business—let's not talk about it. It bores me to tears."

"You should take more interest in Michael and his work."

"But I do. Michael's very sweet."

"The exact opposite of Phillip Blazer," Kelly said pointedly.

"Are you implying that's the only reason I'm dating him?"

"Maybe," Kelly said. "I think it's a lousy stunt to be pulling on Michael."

"I see you're not in the best of moods," Angela said, getting into a quick huff. "See you around."

She left Kelly sputtering behind her and quickly walked out of the school. By the time she had driven back to Casa Linda, she knew Kelly, as usual, had put a finger on the exact spot. Maybe Kelly was right about Michael. But at least he was a pleasant diversion, and that was all she wanted right now.

There was a storm brewing out on the Gulf. She could feel it but not yet see it. It was like that on Bella Grande sometimes. Eventually there would come a hush when the gulls stopped squawking and then, with a kind of eerie swiftness, the rain and wind would hurtle against the beach. Usually it blew out as swiftly as it came.

Most houses were secured behind private courtyards and Angela was soon turning in at the gates of Casa Linda, screeching tires as she came to a halt. She hurried inside.

The hall was a cool terrazzo, the walls plastered in a rough, swirling design and painted a mint green. It opened into a large living room with one wall of sliding glass doors which led outside. In the other direction was a study where Edward Wales often worked nights, a worried fur-

13

row in his forehead, and beyond that there was a second hall leading to another wing of the house where bedrooms opened to the sea, as well as a private garden and a small swimming pool.

"Emma!" Angela called.

Angela went in search of the housekeeper and found her in the guest room working swiftly, almost anxiously.

"What's up?" Angela said.

"Your father phoned half an hour ago. We're having an overnight guest."

"Oh, great!"

Her father often played host to visiting officials of the company. Most of the time they were dull men who smoked smelly cigars, drank too much, and when Edward Wales wasn't looking, made quick passes at his daughter. Angela was adept at staying just out of their reach.

"Which one this time? I hope it's not that awful Mr. Peabody."

"New one. Never heard his name before."

"I'm going to work in the darkroom awhile. If I don't, I'll never have those blow-ups ready for the show—"

"Don't get involved for long. Your father specifically wants you at dinner to meet his guest."

Angela muttered a few choice words under her breath. Sometimes her father, for all she loved him, had a domineering way that rubbed her the wrong way.

"Humor him," Emma said. "He needs you, Angela."

"But why?" Angela burst out angrily. "I know he seems more involved with the office lately—but Emma, I'm not a little bauble on his watch chain to dangle in front of his stuffy business acquaintances!"

Emma gave her an indulgent smile. "Michael has gone and your father knew he was leaving, so what can it hurt to humor him tonight?"

Emma could be very persuasive and Angela felt herself weakening.

"The things I do because you talk me into them. If there's no time for work in the darkroom, I hope there is time for a swim."

14

"Your father said he'd meet the plane about seven and we'd have dinner at eight."

Minutes later, Angela, wearing a bikini that showed off the trim, slender lines of her body, along with all the right curves, dove into the aquamarine of the swimming pool and touched the bottom before she sprang back up, shaking the water from her face. She loved the pool, was expert at diving, and probably could swim faster than any of her friends, men and women alike.

"I think I've sired a mermaid," was the way her father always teased her. "And such a lovely one, too."

She swam back and forth the length of the pool, pushing harder and harder, as if in strict training. It was a way to work off steam, to abate the restlessness and dread of the long, dull evening she had ahead of her. She missed the fun and excitement of New York City and she missed Phillip. She'd always told Kelly that the way to forget one man was to find another. But somehow Michael was not quite doing that for her.

She was just climbing out of the pool when Emma came to speak with her again.

"Angela, your father just phoned. He's been delayed at the office. He wants you to drive out to the airstrip and meet Mr. Stevens. The plane is due in forty-five minutes. You'd better hurry."

"Can't they send a company car for him?"

Emma wouldn't argue or speculate, but went to prepare Angela's bath and asked what she wanted to wear.

"The green."

"The blue is better."

"The green, Emma!"

Emma took the flimsy green dress off the hanger and laid it on the bed with a disapproving frown.

When Angela dressed twenty minutes later, she viewed herself in the mirror. The green dress showed off her tanned shoulders, her pulsing throat, the sparkling burnish of her dark hair, her small rounded chin, her flashing blue-, almost violet-colored eyes, and her even white teeth. Her smile ended with a dimple at the corner of her mouth.

Emma scowled, eyeing the low-cut dress. "Do you think your father will approve?"

"Just because I have to be bored with some old fogy tonight, I don't have to dress like some old maid. What's this man's name?"

"Shawn Stevens. You're to bring him straight to the house and your father will probably be here from the office by the time you get back."

No one interesting from Banner Oil had ever been their house guest. She dreaded the evening and wondered if she could steal away early for some work in her darkroom. She wished Kelly had agreed to come. She wished . . .

"Oh, damn!" she sighed. "I'm stuck and I might as well make the best of it."

At the airstrip there wasn't a company plane in sight. Maybe there had been bad weather somewhere and Shawn Stevens had been delayed. She paced about impatiently, watching the skies, listening for the sound of aircraft. All she could hear was some kind of racket inside the hangar. One of the company mechanics must be working late.

The right engine of a small twin-engined plane was being attacked furiously by a man in greasy coveralls as he swayed rather precariously back and forth on a ladder propped against the wing.

"Hey!" Angela called. "You up there—"

The man stared down at her, obviously annoyed at the interruption. A pair of hazel eyes with gold flecks flashed at her from under heavy brows. A lock of dark hair had fallen to his forehead, where a smudge of grease matched the one on his cheek.

"Blasted carburetor! I've tinkered and tinkered and it still runs ragged."

She had never seen this mechanic before. He must be new to the island. He came quickly down the ladder and thrust the flashlight into her hand. "Beam it right up there, will you?"

"Look, I didn't come out here to hold a light for you!"

"Dammit, hold it still, will you?"

"I've better things to do. It seems our big-shot guest isn't going to show. Some manners!"

With that she thrust the light back into the mechanic's hands and walked away. Finding a phone, she called her father at the office.

"How long do I have to wait?" she asked. "There's no one here."

"But Shawn phoned half an hour ago and said he'd wait for you there," he said with surprise.

"There's no one here but a greasy, bossy mechanic—"

She spun around. The "mechanic" stood there grinning at her. He leaned in the doorway, a devilish twinkle in his eyes. Angela turned back to the phone.

"Never mind, Dad. I found him."

She hung up and faced the arrogant stranger. "You could have told me who you were, you know!"

"Big-shot guest, am I?"

"I'll be driving back to Casa Linda now. If you're coming—"

"Give me a minute, will you?" he asked with a lifted brow. "You want me to go looking like this?"

He disappeared into the darkening hangar and she shouted after him, "Five minutes or you can walk!"

Five minutes was ample. He returned in a gray suit, tall, lithe, with the shoulders of a football player. He had a strong face and eyes that challenged her. Thick lashes curled up boyishly, but his chin was hard. His mouth was all roguish male.

"So, you're Edward Wales's daughter," he said. "Interesting . . ."

Angela walked out of the hangar ahead of him and he followed at a leisurely pace, but his steps were so swift that he kept abreast of her. He tossed his things into the back of Michael's small car and got in beside her. His legs were so long that he had to sit with his knees hunched up.

"I assume I've wrecked your evening somehow," he said.

Her lips lifted in a cool smile. "None of your business."

She gave him a ride to remember, putting Michael's car through paces it had never attempted, speeding down straightaways, stopping and starting quickly, and taking corners with squealing wheels. Shawn Stevens didn't turn a hair.

At Casa Linda she played the hostess to the hilt, leading him into the house, showing him the guest room, and inviting him into the living room for a drink.

"What will it be?" she asked.

"Scotch and water will do nicely."

She fixed it and pushed the drink into his waiting hand with a too-sweet smile.

"Now, if you'll excuse me, I'm sure Dad will be along shortly. Please give him my apologies, but I won't be joining you for dinner."

Dad would rave and snort, but let him.

Shawn laughed softly and tasted the drink, the ice rattling in the glass.

"Dinner won't last forever," he said. "Maybe we could go out later and you could show me the sites of Bella Grande."

"Sorry. I'm busy."

"Pity," he said and his eyes were mocking her again. "But I'll be seeing you again, Miss Wales. Count on it."

Chapter II

Angela left Shawn with a turn of her heel and a flit of her skirt. She took refuge in her darkroom at the rear of the garage, a small place she had outfitted while still in school and pressed into service again now that she was home. Here the smell of the developers didn't reach the main part of the house and she was assured of privacy. Flipping on the red light outside the door as she went in, she reached for a rubber apron which she put over her dress. It was insane to be out here dressed like this, but she was too angry to change to something more suitable. Let Shawn Stevens cool his heels alone! She hoped Dad kept him waiting an hour or more.

When the red light was on, it indicated that she was in the midst of developing her film, and no one was allowed to enter the room. She was surprised when someone pounded at the door.

"Your father is here and he's very upset," Emma called.

"Sorry, Emma. I have to do these prints."

"He's truly upset!" Emma wailed.

Angela nearly weakened but then shook her head. "Go back and serve dinner, Emma. If there's anything left over, I'll come by the kitchen a little later."

Emma finally went away and Angela began to breathe easier. She worked for more than two hours, watching her prints come to life, pleased with most of them, especially those of José Hagar. What a priceless subject he was!

When she looked at the fruits of her labor hanging by clips to dry, she wished for a moment that Phillip Blazer could see them. No matter what their differences, Phillip knew good photography when he saw it and she felt certain he would like her work.

She had invited some of her old friends from New York to attend her show. She didn't expect any of them to come, but she had told Janice Holt about it, and Janice would run like a deer to tell Phillip. She felt her face go warm at the way she had used her old acquaintance, but then, all's fair, she told herself.

When the developing was done, she studied the dried prints until she was satisfied that she had enough photographs to round out the group for next week's show. She flipped off the lights and walked around the house toward the yellow glow from the kitchen windows. Just to the west the surf slushed against the sand and the air hung warm and oppressive. A flash of lightning cut across the distant sky.

Emma was tidying the kitchen for the night, looking tired and out of sorts.

"Any leftovers?" Angela asked brightly.

"You'll have to get them yourself," Emma said peevishly.

"Mad at me?"

"You acted like a spoiled brat."

Angela's temper flared right back. "Correction. I acted like an individual."

She raided the refrigerator, made herself a sandwich of thick-sliced beef, added some of Emma's exquisite salad, and ended her supper with a healthy slice of cheesecake.

"Such food, Emma! I'll gain ten pounds."

Emma scowled, but she was softening.

"Really, Emma, wasn't it better for Dad to be able to talk over dinner and have the business done? If I'd been present, they'd have made polite conversation until coffee in the study—and then it would have been all hours before he could go to bed."

Emma sighed. "Angela Wales, ever since you were a small tike you've known how to talk yourself around me."

Angela laughed and gave Emma a quick hug and kiss. "You've been like a mother to me, you know, ever since Mother died—even before that. It was always you that I came to when things went wrong. Mother wasn't home or she was napping, or she just couldn't be bothered."

"Just the same, I wish you'd see your father before you go to bed," Emma countered.

"All right."

It was not a promise she wanted to keep, but she did. There was a light in the study but no sound of voices. Peering in, she found her father alone behind his desk, poring over a stack of papers.

"Dad—"

He looked up, slowly took off his horn-rimmed glasses, and tossed them aside. His graying hair was ruffled, as if he'd been running his hands through it, and there seemed to be new lines of fatigue around his mouth.

"Come in, Angela. I must talk with you."

"Still angry?"

He shook his head. "Disappointed. But I owe you an apology. I shouldn't expect you to drop everything on such short notice. Forgive me?"

"I'm afraid I wasn't very nice to our guest. Is Shawn all settled?"

"Yes. What happened between you two anyway? I've never known you to do this before."

"It doesn't matter. Who is he, Dad?"

"Just another company man."

But he made it sound too casual, too unimportant. A little warning light came on inside her head.

"How are things coming for your show?" he asked.

"I got the last of the photos today. Of José, who else? I'll do the blow-ups tomorrow."

"What about your New York friends?"

"I doubt if they'll come—things are always so hectic there, you know. Now, if there's peace between us, I'm for bed. Lots of work to do tomorrow."

"See you for breakfast?" he asked hopefully.

She smiled. "Sure. I'll try."

She said a quick good night. Passing Shawn's room, she saw a light under his door and wondered if he represented some kind of danger to her father, who seemed more anxious about his house guest than usual.

Angela couldn't sleep. After an hour of tossing and turning she gave up in despair and went to stand by the window. The air had turned cooler at last, but still seemed heavy and close. Tugging on a flimsy negligee, tying the silk ribbon at her throat, and poking her toes into a pair of mules, she went out through the sliding glass doors to the garden patio. Not a leaf stirred. Looking toward the ocean, she saw that the stars had been blotted out. She anticipated the upcoming storm with a kind of nervous but anxious need. A clash of thunder came moments later. She listened as it rumbled across the sky and then felt the first stirring of sea air across her face. Suddenly she was aware of something else—cigarette smoke. Shawn had come out of his room as well. In a flash of lightning she saw him, tall and male, his shoulders wide beneath a satin robe. His cigarette glowed again.

"So, you couldn't sleep either," he said. His voice was low and reached out to her, drawing her full attention, but she was still angry with him for the stunt he had pulled at the airfield. There was something else as well. Her father's obvious feeling about the man extended to her. She didn't trust him.

"Is it going to storm?" he wondered out loud.

He strode toward her with a grace that made her think of a sleek, prowling panther. He was very tall, taller than she had first thought. She was aware of her own small size as he came to stand beside her, her head barely reaching his shoulder. He flipped his cigarette out into the darkness, the red sparks dying before they dropped to the sand.

"I rather like a storm," he said. "It clears the air."

"Does it?" she asked crisply.

He laughed softly. "Sore as hell, aren't you? Where's your sense of humor, Miss Wales?"

She hated to admit that in a way it had been funny. He thrust his hands into the pockets of his robe.

"Seems we got off on the wrong foot. Should I apologize? Will that help?"

"It will do for starters," she said.

A gust of wind pushed across the Gulf toward them. It felt cool and refreshing against Angela's face. She looked up to see the clouds rolling in, revealed by the thrust of increasingly brilliant lightning.

"Do you want to go back inside?" he asked.

She lifted her chin. "Storms don't frighten me."

"I see."

"They've never frightened me. Not even as a little girl."

"I've a hunch there's not much that does frighten you," he said with a touch of wryness.

She ignored it. The storm was fascinating to watch as it began to grow in intensity.

"So, you're a serious photographer," Shawn said. "At least so your father tells me."

"You needn't sound so surprised."

"Brains and beauty, all bundled up in one little woman," he said "My, my!"

She clenched her fists. She itched to put him in his place again, but there was no time to think about it, for she saw an aluminum lawn chair go hurtling into the darkness snatched up by the wind. She ran after it, the wind tearing in earnest at her negligee and tangling her hair as the first few splatters of rain struck her face.

Then Shawn was beside her. taking the chair from her hands. His fingers covered hers warmly for a second or two and she was suddenly and acutely aware of him.

"I think we'd better make everything fast," he said. "I have a hunch this old girl means business."

The wind was coming in gusts and Angela hurried to collect the rest of the lawn furniture, placing it safely near the garage. One of Emma's prized potted geraniums teetered precariously on a table and both of them dashed for it. They reached it at the same time and Angela had a pleasant sensation of colliding with a long length of well-muscled thigh and a hard chest. Shawn put his arm out and caught both her and the flowerpot. They rocked unsteadily for a moment, regaining their balance. Shawn laughed.

"We'd better get closer to the house before we're blown away, too!" he shouted.

He sheltered her as they ran back, but the rain was coming in torrents now, so they stopped under the patio awning, where she deposited the geranium safely out of the weather. The rain still swept against them, but they were out of the worst of it.

"How long will this downpour last?" Shawn asked.

"On the island no two storms are ever alike."

"Like women," he murmured.

"Funny how men always put everything into the female gender."

He grinned, shaking the rain out of his eyes. "Perfectly natural," he said.

His arm brushed hers and she was alarmed to realize that a little tingle went chasing along her nerves. A particularly harsh clap of thunder filled the air around them.

"Don't you think we should make a run for the house? Can't you watch from there?"

They were far from sheltered or dry where they were, but she shook her head.

"Go if you like. I'm staying a little while longer—"

"So, you're hung up on storms."

"You needn't make it sound like I'm some kind of loony."

He laughed softly. "Just trying to get a fix on you, Angela."

"I've always wanted to photograph a storm, step by step. But it seems the best ones come at night. It's very difficult to capture anything then. Still, there should be some way . . ."

She broke off, not wanting to bore him with the technique of shooting film. She was certain he couldn't care less. The storm was surely at its peak now. But even the sharper lightning and the harsher thunder didn't drive her inside.

"You really do plan to stay here and drown, don't you?" he asked. "You might take a chill."

Her clothes were wet and sticking to her, outlining every enticing curve, and with a rush of warmth, she realized Shawn wasn't missing any of it. That decided her.

"Good night, Mr. Stevens," she said.

She started to run back to the safety of the house, but he came with her, taking her arm in a firm grip. They splattered across the puddles on the flagstone walk, brushed the wet leaves of the foliage, and finally reached the sliding glass doors that went into her room. She had expected him to leave her there, but instead, he came rushing in with her.

"Whew! What a rain!" he said.

The room was still hot with pre-storm, pent-up air.

"Mr. Stevens—"

"Your room was closer than mine," he murmured. "Do you mind?"

Then he slid the door shut, imprisoning them together. He was standing much too close to her. She caught his rain-fresh, male scent. It was a spicy fragrance that she knew she'd never forget. She was like that—associating one thing with another. This aroma would conjure up a rainy, stormy night in her darkened bedroom for years to come. And the man—she knew she wouldn't forget him either. The electricity wasn't just outside. It was in the room, too.

"Storms bring out the senses, have you ever noticed?" he asked quietly. "Everything's sharper, sweeter—"

The rain was hammering nervously at the door. In the flashes of lightning, she found his eyes studying her with a more than curious look. There was a feeling of loneliness about him, a kind of terrible hunger and need.

"I think you'd better say good night," she said.

But he didn't move. "How do you do it, Angela?" he asked. "How can you look absolutely enchanting when you should look like a drowned kitten?"

He reached out and brushed back a lock of her wet hair. His palm brushed her cheek and his touch seemed to set off her pulse until it caught for a moment in her throat, then broke loose and ran fast again.

"Stirs you up, doesn't it?" he asked.

"Shawn—"

He was moving in closer now, swallowing up that very precarious distance between them.

"Blame it on the storm," he said. "Besides, you want it too, Angela. I've tuned in to your radar, my sweet."

"This is ridiculous!"

"This is the way it goes, honey. It happens like this sometimes."

"No—"

But then he was so near she could feel the warmth of his body and she couldn't seem to move. With a rush he pulled her into his arms in an anxious, urgent way. Then he held her against him for a long while, as if savoring the moment. She felt oddly protected in his arms and then he leaned back to bend his head low.

"Angela," he whispered.

His lips touched her wet hair, and then her hot forehead, and lingered momentarily on her eyelids.

"Ah, yes," he said.

Then against her will, her arms reached up to pull his head down further still, so that his mouth could find hers. The kiss was deep, searching, and for a moment she couldn't seem to wrest away. Then with a laugh he let her go and held her at arm's length, as if to study her. She tried to escape him.

"Nowhere to run," he said.

"Let me go!"

"Must I?"

"Yes!"

He released her with a reluctant air. "We might go back out and walk in the rain. We're both already soaked."

She reached out to switch on a lamp, but his hand clamped around her wrist. "Let's keep it this way."

"Mr. Stevens—"

"Under the circumstances, I think you can call me Shawn." His voice was maddeningly amused now, as if this was only a pleasant pastime.

"I'd like you to leave now, Shawn," she said tightly.

"And have me get drenched all over again?"

"You can reach your room by going down the hall."

"Your father might see me leaving. How could I explain that?"

"You're impossible!"

"You're not so bad yourself," he retorted quickly.

With an angry gesture, she broke free of his hold on her wrist and snapped on the lamp. They blinked at each other in the sudden brightness. He leaned back against the glass door, his arms folded across his chest, and stared at her with admiration. She felt another flush come to her face and quickly went to snatch a dry robe out of her closet. She pulled it on and opened her door.

"Out," she said.

He stayed where he was.

"Must I call my father?"

He grinned and it infuriated her all the more. "You wouldn't."

"Want to try me?"

He shrugged. "Okay, I'll go. The least you could do is offer your guest a cup of hot tea to ward off the chills. Or a hot toddy."

"And if I don't?"

He paused beside her, his hand against her warm face, his fingers reaching up to tangle in her damp hair. His presence was overpowering. In a moment, his mouth would be on hers again. She pulled away and stepped out into the hall.

"The kitchen's this way."

He followed, walking silently behind her. They had decided against tea and settled for milk instead. She felt as if the storm had thrown her emotions completely out of control, out of context with her personality. No man had ever maneuvered her so swiftly into his arms.

"Is there any of that super dessert left?" he wondered.

She pushed the last piece of Emma's cheesecake, liberally covered with fresh strawberries, toward him. He polished it off quickly.

"I was hungry," he said with a shrug. "I'm always hungry."

His gaze wandered lazily and warmly over her, lingering for a long time on the soft spot of her throat.

"If you think you can survive now until breakfast, I'll say good night," she said crisply.

"Storm's not over."

He had no sooner said it than the lights blinked, dimmed, and then went out, leaving them in total darkness. At her gasp, he reached out to her, finding her at last.

"Don't be afraid."

"I'm never afraid!"

"Then why are you trembling?" he asked.

"Mr. Stevens—Shawn—will you kindly let go of me?"

But he wouldn't listen. He pulled her against him and white lightning seemed to bounce around the room in fiery balls, like a Fourth of July rocket gone berserk.

"That hit something!" Shawn said with awe. "Are you all right?"

"Yes, I think so."

They groped their way to the kitchen door and looked out. A palm tree had come down, toppled by wind and lightning. It stretched out like a wounded soldier across the white sand.

"What a shame." Shawn said.

"I loved that old tree!"

"Do you get blows like this very often?"

"This is just a mild storm. You should go through a hurricane."

"No, thank you," he said. Then he turned to her with a grin as the lights came back on. "Unless I could share it with you. I'd go through any old storm with you, Angela."

"I think it's time to say good night."

"And just when I thought things were getting interesting—"

"Don't get the wrong idea, Shawn."

"I've had all the right ideas ever since I saw you earlier tonight at the hangar."

She didn't give him time to elaborate. Instead she

moved away, walking quickly, head up, fighting to bring her nerves under control. All the way back to her room, with Shawn following with long, leisurely strides, she chided herself for being so weak, for letting this happen. Was she so vulnerable? *Oh, Michael, why did you have to desert me tonight of all nights?* Michael, all snug and safe in Chicago—then Phillip Blazer crossed her mind. Even Phillip had not built such a quick and intense fire as Shawn Stevens!

The rain finally stopped and the stars came out, but Angela was wide awake. Fresh air came in through the windows she had opened, and thinking of the beach, rain-washed and clean, she very nearly got up to go for a walk. But it had been a long day in many ways and she finally fell asleep.

It was morning when she awakened to the sound of Emma calling her name.

"Breakfast in half an hour and your father's expecting you to join him and Mr. Stevens," she said.

Shawn! As if struck by a thunderbolt, Angela sat up with a gasp. Last night was all too vivid in her mind. Her face went hot as she remembered their passionate kiss during the storm.

She hurried out of bed, not certain just how she would handle Shawn when she saw him. If he had any ideas of continuing in the same vein, he could just think again! It even crossed her mind to join Michael in Chicago. How his proper brows would go up at the sight of her in his hotel room! She laughed, feeling wicked. But there was too much to keep her here. Her one-woman show was just days away and she wasn't ready for it.

Shawn and her father were waiting for her. Shawn's lazy gaze swept over her in a veiled way and he seemed almost distant now. She was instantly relieved. Perhaps he realized how foolishly they had both acted last night.

"Shawn will be staying with us for a few days, Angela," her father was explaining. "I'm going to be tied up with an important meeting tonight, but perhaps you can take Shawn to the yacht club for dinner."

Alarm raced through her and she fought to keep composed. The last thing in the world she wanted was to be thrown into an evening with Shawn!

"I understand the yacht club is the main source of entertainment on the island," Shawn said smoothly.

She met his hazel eyes. The gold flecks in them seemed to be taunting her, daring her.

"It is. I'm sure you'll enjoy it."

"Then it's settled," her father said happily. "I'll have my secretary make a reservation for you. Say seven?"

Shawn's lips had quirked upward with a devilish grin. "That would be very good," he nodded.

Angela pretended to be busy spreading jam on her toast. Right now she couldn't meet Shawn's eyes. The thought of being with him was at once exciting and dangerous.

"Do you go sailing, Miss Wales?" Shawn asked.

"I'm not crazy about it, but I often go with the crowd. I actually prefer an old flat-bottomed fishing boat that a friend of mine owns."

Her father frowned. He had never quite approved of her relationship with José Hagar. Her mother had abhorred it.

"Nice young ladies don't hang around with old fishermen," she had scolded.

"He's the most interesting, honest, and real person on the island. He's not phony like so many of our so-called friends."

That, of course, had started one of their many arguments. Even now, with her mother gone, Angela sometimes felt guilty about stealing off for an afternoon in José's boat.

Now she defended her old friend to Shawn.

"José is Spanish, handles a boat like no one else, and knows these waters like the back of his hand."

Shawn arched his brow. "I see."

Shawn had immediately jumped to the wrong conclusion.

"He's retired now," Angela said with a deliciously wicked thrust. "He spends his days on the porch watching the surf and drinking coffee, sometimes laced with rye."

Her father cleared his throat awkwardly. "I'm sure, Angela, that Shawn would rather hear about the attributes of our yacht club." He turned the conversation in that direction and Angela smiled to herself. Shawn kept giving her curious, puzzled looks. Her father had been embarrassed and she supposed she should be sorry about that. But Shawn might as well have no illusions about her. In fact it would be a relief if he decided to cancel tonight. The truth was she wasn't sure she could handle him and the thought was unsettling.

As soon as they had driven away to the Banner Oil offices, Angela tried to reach Michael at his Chicago hotel, but he didn't answer.

"Damn!" she murmured.

Hearing Michael's steady voice would have put things back into the right perspective. Now she felt at loose ends. Work waited in the darkroom. She must take care of it or the show would never get off the ground. But what did it really mean to be praised by old friends or Dad's business acquaintances and colleagues, who felt they had to say the right thing? Unless Phillip came . . .

Gooseflesh rippled over her arms. Phillip! But it was useless to think about him or plan on his coming. He wouldn't be caught dead here.

She labored all morning in the darkroom, making huge enlargements of selected prints and staying there until Emma came to tell her that lunch was ready.

Angela ate under the patio awning where she and Shawn had taken refuge the night before. The surf was only a few steps away, rushing hungrily at the white sand.

"Sit down, Emma," Angela said. "Talk to me."

Emma had to be coaxed, but she finally took a chair and they discussed last night's storm. Her father had called someone to come and remove the fallen palm tree.

"It was old. It had had its time," Emma said. "Who rescued my geranium?"

"I did," Angela said.

"Didn't expect such a blow or I'd have brought it in."

The geranium, cradled in her arms, had been caught by Shawn as well. Angela remembered his long, hard body pressed against hers, the way he had shielded her from the rain and wind, protecting her—that sort of thing could easily go to a woman's head.

"Angela—"

"What? What did you say, Emma?"

"Wool gathering again! Honestly, Angela—"

"I've a lot on my mind, Emma. The show, all the work yet to be done, and right this minute, I don't want to do any of it. I think I'll take a walk after lunch."

Emma sighed. "To see José, I suppose."

"Well, at least you don't get in a tizzy about it like everyone else."

"José's a good, honest man. I'm glad you're not a snob, Angela."

The sun was high and bright when Angela walked away from Casa Linda and went down to find José. It was a pleasant stroll and José's weathered cottage was like a haven to her. Everyone on Bella Grande knew José and all remembered his handsome son, who had lived with him until he got married. Then a tragic accident had taken both his son and daughter-in-law away from him, but had given him little Thomasita.

"My life, my sunshine," José had said of her. "What would I do without her?"

Then he had put his fingers to his lips and blown a kiss to the winds.

The heat was already searing and the sand was hot beneath Angela's bare toes. The storm had smoothed the water, eased the tide, and the fishing boats were anchored on the horizon.

In a moment Thomasita materialized and ran to meet Angela, grasping her hand happily and skipping along beside her.

"Why aren't you in school today?" Angela asked.

"I stayed home to help Grandpa. The storm almost sank *Lady!*"

Lady was José's fishing boat in which Angela had spent many a happy hour.

José was on the porch in his old rocker, smoking his

pipe. He grinned at Angela. "I thought you'd be getting ready for your show."

"Don't make me feel guilty! I should be doing that instead of this."

"Fix us something cold to drink, Thomasita," José told his granddaughter.

Angela had always been able to find peace here, but today she squirmed on the wooden step and stirred restlessly.

"So, what's bothering you, Angela?"

She looked up into José's inquisitive face. How well he could read her every mood!

Before she could answer, Thomasita was back, pressing a glass of cold lemonade into her hand. It was sweet and tart with some secret ingredient she had never identified. As usual, she found it satisfying.

They didn't talk now. It was never necessary with José. Thomasita came to sit beside Angela and leaned her head against Angela's knee. She stroked the child's silky black hair. She would like a daughter like this someday, a laughing, sun-kissed girl with flashing eyes.

"So, tell me what's wrong," José asked again.

"Shawn Stevens. Do you know of him?"

"Do you ask for yourself?"

"For Dad!" she said quickly.

José grinned. "Oh! Well, I hear them talking around the island. Stevens is a big wheel from New York."

"How do you always know what's going on at Banner Oil?"

José shrugged. "It's my island. I was here before anybody."

She laughed. "I suppose that's true. How big a wheel is Shawn?"

"Big enough maybe."

"There's something in the wind—"

"Always is. Salt, storms, secret loves, scent of blossoms—"

"Stop being a romantic and tell me."

"I only know that everybody's nervous about his being here."

Angela stirred again and looked at her watch. She must get back. She said quick good-byes. All the way up the beach toward Casa Linda she felt a nagging restlessness, an uncertainty. And there was tonight to look forward to, a taunting, tantalizing situation that could lead . . . she shook her head and thought of other things. Shawn must not become important to her. He was only a passerby—a ship in the night. . . .

Chapter III

The more Angela heard about Shawn Stevens, the more intrigued she was. At first he had struck her as arrogant and cocksure, and she was still burning over the trick he had played on her at the airfield. From the beginning she had sensed he represented danger of some kind, if not to her father, then to herself. The passionate kiss during the storm was only part of it. There was a strange need in the man that she wanted to respond to. Why else would she have done what she had done?

Tonight she would proceed cautiously, play the hostess as her father had asked, and try to remember that Shawn was no one special.

She kept telling herself these things all the time she was selecting one of her loveliest dresses.

It was shortly after five-thirty when she heard Shawn come into the house. A few minutes later as she passed his door she could hear the buzz of his electric shaver.

She made Shawn wait for her a good ten minutes. Then she made an entrance into the living room and saw that the effect was not lost on him. His eyes glowed warmly and his mouth lifted in a pleased smile. She hated to admit that when he smiled like that something seemed to melt inside her bones, robbing her of all her good sense.

"Lovely!" he murmured.

She gave him a little nod. "Thank you."

"And cold as ice," he said, pretending to shiver. "I was hoping we could pick up where we left off last night."

She brushed that remark aside. "I do hope you'll enjoy the club."

He laughed quietly and took her arm. A tingle went along her arm as he touched her, bending his head slightly toward her, the picture of attention.

"I'm sorry we have to keep using your car," he said. "Perhaps I should arrange to rent one."

"It's quite all right. But the car isn't mine. Would you like me to drive?"

"No, thanks. I'd prefer to get there alive."

She smiled with satisfaction. So her wild drive from the airstrip last night hadn't been lost on him after all!

He took the wheel with authority, somehow managing to get his long legs inside the little car. He drove swiftly but with care. He darted a glance toward her.

"If this isn't your car, then whom does it belong to?"

"Michael Field."

"Oh, Michael. I see."

"I suppose you know him."

"Casually. Banner Oil is so big, it's impossible to know everyone well. I believe he's off to Chicago right now. I'm glad."

She decided it was best to ignore that remark.

"Is it a serious thing with you and Michael?"

She gave him a cool look. "So, you've been talking about me."

"You're a very popular young lady, it seems. You didn't tell me about your show. When will it be?"

"A week from Thursday."

"Do I get a preview? I probably won't be on Bella Grande more than a few days."

"Are you interested in photography?"

He laughed. "If you saw the pictures I take, you wouldn't have to ask. I always end up with all sky or ceiling, with people's heads cut off, or with half their bodies missing—I'm atrocious at it."

"If photography isn't your long suit, then what is?"

He drove steadily for a moment or two and then tossed

a glance at her, as if testing to see if she was seriously interested or not.

"Flying. I love antique airplanes. Swimming, skiing. Music—certain jazz trumpet players, a ragtime piano. and I enjoy the classics, too. I like the water—I find Bella Grande one of the most enchanting places I've ever been."

"And women?" she murmured dryly.

"Oh, definitely the *femme fatale*," he said with a grin. "But I'm selective. I'm just glad to find that there's a woman like you on the island. I was prepared for some very long and boring days—and nights—and then there you were."

"You're from the New York office. Does that mean you're a native of that state?"

"No. Indiana. I lived in a very small town and my father was an electrical engineer there. We moved around a lot. My dad liked to chase rainbows. He was a free spirit. I always envied him."

He sounded wistful, a little sad. The cheerful cockiness had faded for a moment.

"I take after my mother," he continued. "She is steady, a plodder. with goals in mind. How those two ever got together, I'll never know. She lives in Boston now. She was born there. I see her three or four times a year."

"How did you and Banner Oil get together?"

"Sheer luck. I was at the right place at the right time after college. You used to work in New York too. *Top Fashion Magazine*. Too bad our paths didn't cross sooner."

She quirked an eyebrow at him. "You've certainly been doing your homework."

His glance swept over her and he gave her a slow smile. "I learned long ago that it pays. Is that the club just ahead?"

"Yes."

Shawn left Michael's car in the hands of the attendant and came around to open Angela's door. His fingers closed around hers as he helped her out. Then he tucked her hand under his arm and they went into the club. Angela was aware of the picture they made, both very dark,

Shawn tall, herself petite. Heads turned, eyebrows went up, whispers started.

Everyone knew Angela and spoke to her as she walked past their tables. Many stopped her. There were introductions, the women ogled Shawn openly, but the men seemed stiff and uneasy in his presence. Tension crackled in the air from the moment they entered the room.

The table Angela's father had reserved for them was one of the best in the house. It looked out over the Gulf and the heavy drapes had not yet been drawn to shut out the night. Mulberry stains were smudged against the sky as well as old lavender and one last crimson streak. Then black began to settle down like folds of velvet and before they had tasted their first cocktails, a lone star had emerged to wink at them.

"One question to clear the air," Shawn said, "which you avoided answering earlier. How serious is it with Michael?"

"Who said it was serious at all?"

His lips lifted into a roguishly handsome smile. He raised his glass. "Cheers. That's what I wanted to hear."

"It can't matter to you!"

A scowl cut across his forehead and he looked at her steadily for a moment. "Contrary to what many think of me, Angela, I'm an honorable man and I have my ethics."

"In business?"

"Also in the affairs of the heart," he said with a slow grin. "But I see you doubt that."

"I don't trust you, Mr. Stevens."

The waiter arrived for their order. Shawn gave their selections with a kind of charm and grace that equaled Phillip Blazer's, perhaps even surpassed his. And she had thought there was no other man in the world like Phillip!

"We shouldn't be wasting the music, Angela," he said. "Shall we?"

They left their table, hand in hand. His arm went around her, he pulled her close, and it was difficult to keep her head from resting on his broad shoulder. He danced very well, moving her around with ease, and she knew that every eye in the place was on them.

"Later will you show me the club? I think a stroll around the yacht basin might be fun," he said.

His eyes met hers and held her gaze. She nearly missed a step.

"You are a bewitching woman, Angela Wales," he said. "I've had trouble concentrating at work today because of you."

"Is this all part of your practiced charm?" she asked as flippantly as she could.

He laughed as he spun her around. "I'm also painfully truthful. It's not a lie, Angela."

She didn't believe him for a moment and was curious as to what else he would say. But she saw that their food was arriving at the table.

He took her back, keeping his arm casually around her waist. Out of the corner of her eye, she saw Brenda Davis staring at them Brenda was the cattiest of the Banner Oil wives. Angela knew that she and Shawn would be the main topics of conversation the next day.

The food was tasty, elegantly served, and Shawn ate with his usual appetite, not even trying to hide his surprise.

"You've a delightful chef here!" he exclaimed.

"So, Bella Grande is not quite as antiquated as you expected."

"You've caught me out. I was expecting the worst. But I've never tasted better veal scallopini. And those crusty rolls—by the way, can you cook?"

She laughed at the unexpected questions. "No. I leave such business to chefs like André here at the club and to Emma. Being a bachelor—by the way, you are a bachelor—"

His gaze burned against her and his lips made a straight line. "You know damned well I am."

She flushed. "All right, so I asked Dad. I thought we were talking about cooking. Are you just a helpless male in the kitchen?"

"My menu consists of about half a dozen dishes. I do eggs pretty well. I'd like to cook breakfast for you sometime."

There was, no doubt, a double meaning to his words, Angela thought. She lifted her chin and ignored them. He laughed softly, but the moment passed.

The food had vanished and Shawn signaled the waiter.

"Coffee, laced with brandy," he said.

The coffee was poured into fragile cups and the candle flickered lower on the table, making intricate patterns across the white linen. Shawn's eyes missed nothing as his gaze dwelt for long moments on the soft hollow of Angela's throat, her full lips, her silky hair. Her senses were aroused against her will. He smoked one cigarette and then another, and when the coffee and the brandy were gone, he pushed his cup aside.

"You promised me a tour of the club," he said.

He took her arm as they left the table and she led the way to a balcony that carried them out over the water. The air was warm, still sweet from the storm. The surf came sloshing in with its rhythmical music. His sleeve brushed her bare arm. Then his hand reached out and found its way beneath the mane of her hair and his fingers caught for a moment.

"Angela—"

"Don't, Shawn!"

"That's a word that isn't in my vocabulary, Angela. Come here, darling. You know you want to."

His arms were around her in a flash and she was suddenly being held firmly and warmly. She thought of a dozen smart and caustic things to say, but none of them would go past her lips. His kiss whispered across her forehead and then with a laugh he suddenly lifted her up in his big hands. Her feet left the floor of the balcony and he held her easily at eye level.

"You're so darned tiny, Angela."

Then, as he held her in mid-air, he leaned toward her and his mouth found hers. A tingling sensation rippled over her and she tried to be free of him, but it seemed her knotted fists gave way to hands that caressed his shoulders and held him closer. Then, as the kiss ended, he let her go slowly and she slid down the long length of his body until her feet touched the floor again. Still, he held her.

"I think we'd better go in," she said.

"Must we? I find this very pleasant."

"Yes, we must."

She moved away from him then and went back toward the sound of music and the murmur of laughter. She had barely put a foot in the door, with Shawn treading quietly behind her, than Harvey Davis bore down on her. Harvey was Brenda's husband and he considered himself the life of the party. With a wife like Brenda, Angela could see why he constantly played up to other women.

"Hello there, my little angel," he said. "This dance is mine. You don't care, do you, Stevens?"

Shawn stiffened. "And if I did—"

Harvey ignored him and whisked Angela away. He swung her around and around, beaming at her with open adoration. Harvey was a dancing fool. Despite everything else about him that Angela found just short of repulsive, she did like to dance with him. Harvey knew every step and every dance and he liked nothing better than making an exhibition of himself, claiming the center of the floor, everyone else off to the sidelines to watch him perform.

Angela caught a glimpse of Shawn at the bar with a drink in his hand. He was tense and angry. All at once she wanted to make him jealous. She shook her hair and slapped her hands together. Harvey laughed.

"Let's show them how to do it, angel baby!"

Angela threw her head back with a delighted laugh and joined in Harvey's madcap dancing. Soon everyone was clapping their hands and calling to them. Angela danced as she had never danced before, letting the music possess her. Harvey howled with delight and called to her and kept right on dancing, shouting to the orchestra to keep playing.

Shawn was still watching and it seemed the longer he stared, the angrier he became. A ramrod seemed to have been shoved up his back, holding his shoulders all the more straight and rigid.

At last Angela held up her hands, out of breath.

"Enough, enough, Harvey! I can't dance another step."

She collapsed in Harvey's arms to a round of applause.

Then Harvey led her off the floor. Suddenly Shawn was there, a tall, lean girder of steel.

"I think we should be going, Angela," he said.

Harvey began protesting. "This was just the first round. After we catch our breath . . ."

"I'd like to leave now, Angela," Shawn said firmly.

Harvey took offense. He was one of those fools who rush in where angels fear to tread.

"Look, Stevens. At Banner Oil you're top dog. This is another matter. Maybe the lady doesn't want to go."

On the sidelines Angela saw Brenda stiffen and motion to her husband to be still. But Harvey ignored her.

"By the way, this is a private club," Harvey said pointedly.

Shawn flushed. Angela saw his fists double up and she moved quickly to his side and took his arm.

"Nice dance, Harvey," she said. "But we really do have to go now. Good night."

She propelled Shawn out of the Yacht club. Once the fresh air hit their faces they paused.

"Sorry about that," he said. "Is Davis always such a loudmouth?"

"When he's drunk a little too much. Tomorrow he'll be properly contrite and apologetic."

Shawn was still angry and Angela sensed it went deeper than Harvey Davis. There was something more.

Once they were in the car Shawn relaxed. He lighted a Belair and held it out to her. She took one long drag and handed it back.

He started the car and drove away with a spin of the wheels. He was gripping the wheel tightly now, driving very fast, his eyes on the road, his mind a hundred miles away.

"My God, Harvey got your goat!" Angela exclaimed with a surprised laugh.

He set his jaw and looked at her. "I've a feeling I'm not very well liked on the island."

42

"Why?"

"Lot's of reasons."

She remembered her father's worried air and she sensed that Shawn Stevens represented the enemy camp.

"Do you let your hair down like that very often?" Shawn asked with a wry smile.

"Only when I'm in the mood."

"Are you in the mood for a walk on the beach?"

"I'm always in the mood for that."

"Good. Where can I park the car?"

She pointed out a bumpy lane just ahead that led down to a clump of palmetto. From there they could reach the beach easily. Michael's little car thumped along and came to a bouncy halt.

The sky was serene, dotted with stars, and the water lay calm with barely a ripple aginst the sand.

"Not like last night," Shawn said, coming around to take her hand and tug her out of the car.

Angela didn't want to think or talk about last night, but his fingers around hers told her that he was remembering.

She hurried on ahead of him, pausing to kick off her shoes. Shawn put his arm around her shoulders as they walked along. The water tickled Angela's feet and rushed over Shawn's shoes.

"Damn!" he said.

"Take them off. Go baerfoot. Be a kid again."

In a moment, he had pulled off his shoes and socks and rolled up the legs of his trousers.

"I feel like Huck Finn."

"No straw hat," she said.

In another moment he had shucked off his white coat, loosened his bow tie, and tossed both of them to the sand.

"Do you swim in the Gulf?" he asked.

"Occasionally. More often at the pool at the club or at home in the pool."

"Don't you like the salt water?"

"The currents are tricky here. I'm always cautious."

"Always?" he asked in a low, meaningful voice. "In everything?"

"My one extravagance is film," she replied.

He laughed. "Film!"

"I waste more than I save. But I always want to be sure I have the shot I want."

"Do you see everything through the eye of a camera?"

"Nearly everything," she said with a nod of her head. "Even tonight at dinner, watching the shadows of the candle—I wanted to capture it on film, the white linen, the wine glass, the cuff of your shirt—your hand—"

"My hand!"

"Very masculine, you know. Exquisitely male."

"I have a feeling I should say thank you."

"Hands tell their own stories. José says he's worked with them all his life, hard work with ropes and nets and traps. Dad's hands are soft and well cared for and look naked without a pen or pencil. Emma's hands are plump and warm—like the bread she bakes and the pillows she fluffs."

He caught her hand and held it up to study it in the starlight. "And what about your own?"

She pulled away from him. "Nothing—"

"No thoughts about your own hands?"

"I'm never pleased. The fingers aren't long enough. They're too small. I always break a fingernail at some inopportune time."

He lifted her hand again and put it against his cheek. "I think it feels just right," he murmured.

For a moment, they stood very close, the water around their feet, and in another second, she was going to be in his arms. She couldn't handle that just now. With a laugh she turned and began to run away, pounding along the beach in her bare feet, her dark hair flying.

"Why you—you imp—" he muttered.

He came after her. She knew he let her stay ahead for a little while, then suddenly he was only a step behind her, with his arms around her in a flying tackle, and he brought her down. They landed together in the sand, laughing and gasping for breath.

"Don't you know you can't escape me, Angela?" he asked.

He was hovering just above her, blotting out the sight of the stars. His warm breath touched her face and then his mouth came down on hers, and against her will her arms went around his neck. The kiss lasted for a long, long time, a searching, anxious kind of kiss.

At last he let her go. He rolled away from her and stretched out on his back. He was so quiet that she raised up on her elbow to look at him. He extended his arm to touch her and she lay down closer beside him, her head on his shoulder.

"I've known you in some other time," he said.

"I don't believe in that."

"Don't knock it. I'm trying to be romantic," he said with a laugh.

"You're doing a pretty good job of it."

"Am I?"

"I don't know just how you did it. No man has ever had me lolling about in the sand in the middle of the night after meeting him just twenty-four hours earlier."

"Seems longer. I meant it when I said I'd known you somewhere before."

"Poppycock!"

"Dammit, will you stop that?" he asked. He pulled her closer and half turned to face her. He ran his lips lightly over her face, as if exploring her, studying her, committing her to memory. She told herself to stop him. This was madness. With a sigh she pulled his head to her, found his lips, and buried herself there in the passion of his mouth.

His kiss became demanding, more eager and hungry. He pulled her closer until she fit the mold of his body and with her breath caught, she clung to him.

The tide had been slowly creeping in. When a splash of water came up over Angela's legs, she jumped with surprise.

"Good heavens! Shawn—"

He was laughing softly. "Who cares?"

"I care. I don't want to get soaking wet—"

"It seems that's our style, honey. Last night it was the storm, tonight it's the tide."

But it was just as well that the tide had brought her to her senses. She leaped up, brushing away the wet sand.

"It's late. I have to go home."

"Now?"

"Yes."

He drew a long breath and reached up a hand to her. "Okay."

She ignored his hand. If she touched him again. . . . Ribbons of fire shot through her at the thought. He got up unassisted.

"How about going swimming with me tomorrow?" he asked. "Here or in your pool or wherever you say—"

"If I can work it in."

He lifted her chin with a finger. "You will," he said quietly.

She trembled, but didn't move an inch toward him. Instead she walked on toward the car, and in a moment he followed.

They retrieved their belongings as they went, Shawn's shoes perilously close to being washed out to sea.

They drove home, quiet now. Shawn drove too fast. When his tires squealed on a particularly sharp curve, Angela sent him an angry look.

"I don't know what's eating you, Shawn Stevens," she said, "but it's no excuse for driving like a maniac."

"How would you know?" he asked. "Do you have any idea what you've done to me tonight, Angela Wales?"

"Nothing," she said firmly.

"I haven't felt as keyed up and excited in—well—months," he said. "I wasn't looking forward to Bella Grande. Now I find it has all kinds of delightful surprises. It has you, Angela."

"Don't ever count on me. I'm the sort that bends with the wind. This is just a stopover for me. After the show—who knows. I may go back to New York. I may try California. I might even just go over to Miami. Don't count on me."

"But I do."

Casa Linda waited in the night behind the courtyard walls, and as Shawn brought the car to a halt, a silence came between them, a poignant moment when Angela found she longed for the night to end on one hand, and hated to give it up on the other.

Her father was at home. A light burned in the study. His important meeting had ended. She wondered what it was all about and why Shawn hadn't mentioned it. Now that she thought of it, he seldom spoke of the company or what he did there. He had never hinted at his reason for coming in the first place.

The moment their steps sounded in the hall, Angela's father called to her. She was glad, for it meant no final moment of parting with Shawn, no chance for him to kiss her again.

When Angela went into the study, he handed her a slip of paper. "Message for you. You're to call back, no matter what the hour. How did you and Shawn enjoy the evening?"

Shawn appeared then. "Very much. How was the meeting?"

Her father's shoulders had dropped. "About as we expected."

Angela called good night to them both and hurried away. The phone call had been from Michael. Seeing his name written on the paper brought her down to earth with a thump. Dear, sweet Michael, with his heart in his eyes. If he had seen her tonight—she shuddered at her behavior. It had started out as a game, a wicked little scheme to put Shawn Stevens in his place. What had happened?

Her head was beginning to ache when she reached her room and put the call in to Michael's Chicago hotel. She braced herself for the sound of his voice.

He answered the first ring.

"Hello, Michael, I'm sorry I missed your call."

"Where in thunder have you been? It has to be past two o'clock in Bella Grande!"

"Yacht club, entertaining one of father's guests. You know how it is, Michael—"

There was a pause and she sensed that something was wrong.

"Michael, what is it? What is so urgent?"

"I've had the rug jerked out from under me. It's not official, but it's in the works. I'm going to be transferred out of Bella Grande."

"What!"

"It all started in the New York office—a big reorganization for the entire company. A man by the name of Stevens . . ."

Angela swallowed hard, the pieces falling into place now, her father's worried air, the hostility toward Shawn at the club tonight . . .

Michael talked on and on and finally, when he had told her all the news and his fears and worries, he confessed that he felt better.

"I need you, Angela. How can I leave you? If I leave Bella Grande, will you come with me, darling?"

"We'll talk later. Let's wait and see what happens."

"All right. Just remember, I love you, Angela."

She murmured good night and hung up.

Angela heard her father call good night to Shawn and go to his room. Immediately after that Shawn's steps came down the hall and his door closed. Moments later there was a tap at Angela's glass door and she found Shawn outside on her patio. She hesitated about opening the door, but she knew he would persist.

"We didn't say good night properly," he said with a burning glance.

"One question," she said, stepping out to the dark beside him.

"Anything."

"Are you responsible for having Michael transferred?"

He stiffened beside her, but didn't answer.

"Did you deliberately—"

He caught her wrist in his big hand and she could feel the heat of his fury.

"You think very highly of me, don't you? You think I use what power I have for self-gratification? You're like the rest of them on this island—you smile to my face and knife me in the back!"

With that, he turned on his heel and stormed away, leaving Angela stunned and surprised.

Chapter IV

Angela avoided Shawn the next morning. When she knew that he and her father had driven to the office, she ate a light breakfast and told Emma she would be busy nearly all day in the darkroom.

"You must take time to eat."

"A sandwich perhaps, some iced tea—give me a shout, will you?"

Emma shook her head, disapproving of the long hours Angela sometimes put in at her work. But the show was only days away and there were still choices to be made. Only so many photographs could be put on display in the small community hall she had rented for the occasion. Her most ardent supporter had been Kelly Ross, but she hadn't seen Kelly since the afternoon she'd stopped by the school. It was her own fault. She had stormed away in a huff over nothing. She barely remembered what they had argued about. Oh, yes, Michael. Kelly constantly defended him.

As always, the hours she spent in the darkroom passed quickly. She was usually able to block out everything else from her mind, but she was annoyed to find that her thoughts frequently strayed to Shawn. Remembering their walk on the beach, she closed her eyes for a moment, a numbing sensation rippling over her. No man had ever set her so on fire so fast.

"Darn it!" she fumed.

She was almost relieved to hear someone knock at her door.

"Red light's on! Can't you see?" she called out.

"I have to speak to you, Angela, when can you come out?" It was Kelly Ross.

"In a minute!"

She opened the door as quickly as she could to find Kelly waiting for her down on the beach, studying the water, kicking at the sand with a thoughtful air.

"What's up?" Angela called.

Kelly came walking quickly toward her, consulting her watch as she came.

"I have only a minute. I'll be late. But how would you like to come to our school picnic on our last day?"

"You're kidding!"

"Kids are sometimes your favorite subjects. I thought you might get some good shots."

"Okay. Maybe I will. When?"

"Friday."

"Day after tomorrow?"

"Yes. And you can have all the picnic food you can eat," Kelly laughed, her blue eyes twinkling.

"I'm not sure I can stand all those noisy kids."

"If I can, you can. See you then?"

"Why not?" Angela asked with a shrug. "It seems everything gets in the way of my finishing the work for the show."

"You must be nearly ready."

"Oh, I suppose so. It's a matter of choice now. I'm having a hard time deciding which photos to eliminate."

Angela walked with Kelly to her car, glad to see that their little differences had been forgotten, as they usually were.

"I'll be free of school by then. I can help you in the hall."

"If you hadn't offered, I was going to shanghai you anyway!"

Kelly drove away with a wave of her hand and disappeared beyond the courtyard gates.

Angela was busy the entire day and when her father

came home from the office, she had just turned out the lights.

"Dear, I'd like to speak with you," he said.

She followed him into the study. "Where's Shawn? Didn't he come with you?"

"Held up at the office. It's Shawn I want to talk about."

"I'm not at all sure he's a favorite subject," she said crisply.

Her father shook his head. "I thought you two were hitting it off. I was hoping you were."

"Is he so important to you?"

"That doesn't matter," her father said quickly. "I'm more concerned with your happiness. I know you seem fond of Michael, but I know, too, that Phillip Blazer is still in your heart."

She laughed and pressed her head to her father's arm for a moment. "You know me too well."

"You were badly hurt," he said. "I'd have been pleased if Michael turned out to be the answer. I'm sure he's a fine young man, but—"

"You mustn't fret about my love life," she told him. "I can handle it. Now what about Shawn?"

"There's to be a company dinner tomorrow night at the hotel in his honor. I'd like you to serve as my hostess."

"Dad, you know how I feel about those things!"

"Humor me," he said with a serious air. "It really is important and God knows you're an asset to any dinner or party."

"Soft soap will get you nowhere," she said dryly. "But if it will make you happy—I'll do my best."

The phone rang on the desk and her father answered it. From the one-sided conversation she could hear, she knew that Shawn was not coming home to dinner. Her father hung up with a scowl.

"It seems he's going to dinner with some of the men from the office."

"What's going on, Dad?"

He shook his head wearily. "A little apple-polishing, I suspect."

Angela was relieved. She could delay the encounter with

Shawn a few more hours. But with Michael away she felt restless and at loose ends. That was the one flaw in Bella Grande. There wasn't enough to do, not after the bright, exciting life in New York City. As soon as the show was behind her, perhaps she should go back to the Big Apple and find some work on some other magazine. If she bumped into Phillip Blazer—she drew a deep sigh. She'd have to bluff it somehow, show him that he had not devastated her after all.

With dinner over, Angela took a drive around the island, watching the sun go down over the horizon, absorbed in the array of colors. She took several shots of it, but sunsets were not easy to capture. When she finally went home, she looked at once to see if there was a light in Shawn's room, but there was none. He was still out.

Her father had shut himself away in the study with a mound of paper work. Angela opted for a swim. Pulling on her bikini, she went out to the pool. The water was still warm from the afternoon sun and she dove in with a splash. She swam for nearly half an hour and when she climbed out, dripping water, tossing off her bathing cap to loosen her hair to the night breezes, she heard a footstep and a beach towel was held out to her by a pair of long arms.

"You swim like there's no tomorrow," Shawn said.

She took the towel, aware that he was eyeing her with interest in the floodlights around the pool, missing none of her curves.

"I'd like to talk to you, Angela."

"I'm not at all certain we have anything to discuss."

He gave her a wry smile. "I owe you an apology. I acted badly last night. I'm sorry."

"As I recall, you didn't answer my question."

"About Michael?"

Angela patted herself dry with the towel and then draped it around her shoulders.

"Yes."

"If Michael is transferred, it is not my doing. There are people over me, you know."

"I don't know what your position is in Banner Oil.

Right now, I don't think I care. Frankly, the company bores me."

Shawn grinned, then broke out into rich laughter. "You're refreshingly frank, aren't you?"

"It seems I've been shackled in one way or another with the blasted Banner Oil Company all my life and it's all anyone ever talks about on Bella Grande! Why wouldn't I be bored?"

"Come and sit down," he said. "We've some fence-mending to do."

"I'll change," she said. "Be back in a moment."

"No need," he said lazily, eyeing her again. "I don't know anyone who looks better in a bikini."

She almost shivered under his gaze, but she didn't linger. Instead, she went back to her room, changed out of the wet suit, and pulled on a pair of slacks and a knit top. When she returned to the pool, Shawn was waiting with two drinks on the wrought-iron table.

He got to his feet. He had changed, too. He looked casual and comfortable in slacks and a knit sport shirt. His broad shoulders slimmed down to narrow hips. His forearms were strong and tanned and she watched as he reached for one of the glasses. "I fixed a drink," he said.

She took it from his hand, her fingers brushing his for a moment, and their gazes locked and held.

"We're melting the ice," she said.

He laughed. "So we are."

They lounged at the table, Shawn's long legs stretched out. His cigarette smoke drifted on the air and he scowled at the bright floodlight.

"Can't we put that out?"

She went to flip a switch, leaving them in darkness. Once her eyes had adjusted she could see him well enough in the light from the house. Ice tinkled in their glasses. He suggested a refill and disappeared, only to return again in a few minutes. He walked easily, quietly.

The second drink disappeared more quickly. He reached out and took her hand.

"We're stalling, you know. Killing time when we both know what we want."

"Do we?" she asked.

She hated it that it suddenly seemed hard to breathe.

"I've thought about you all day, Angela."

"Really?"

His shoulders tensed. "Dammit, why do you put me down? Why do you make it seem as if I'm lying in my teeth!"

She laughed softly. "Maybe just to hear you explode."

He sighed, exasperated, and then he laughed, too. "We could take a walk," he said.

"I don't feel like walking."

"A drive?"

"Around the island? I know the place by heart and believe me, there isn't anything interesting to do at night. Unless you want to go back to the club."

"No. I was there for dinner. But we could go to the mainland."

"I've had a busy day," she countered.

"That busy?"

"I was in the darkroom most of the time."

He leaned away and looked at her through the dim light. "When do I get a preview of your show?"

"When I've decided I'm ready."

He sputtered angrily. "Hell, Angela, what do I have to do to get through to you? What's happened? Last night—"

"Was a mistake," she said quickly.

He set his glass down with a thump and got angrily to his feet. "Do you want to clarify that?"

"I'm impulsive sometimes," she said with a shrug. "I was last night and I shouldn't have been."

"Everything was as smooth as silk until you talked about Michael Field, then you turned on me. Are you in love with him after all?"

She didn't want to discuss Michael with him. Michael was good and decent and he had filled a need in her life. To speak of him in the same breath with Shawn seemed wrong somehow.

"I think I'll just say good night, Shawn."

He stopped her with a hand on her arm. "Don't go in just yet. It's not late."

"Sorry."

"Has your father told you about the dinner at the hotel in my honor?" he asked.

"Yes."

"You'll go with me," he said.

She moved away from him. "I'm afraid not. I'll be acting as hostess for my father, but that's all."

He followed her to the glass doors of her bedroom. She turned back, blocking his way. "You're not going to come in."

He laughed softly, then reached out and touched her hair. His fingers worked magic. She felt an electric charge go through her.

"There will be a moon later," he said.

"Shawn, don't do this."

"I must," he murmured. "I must."

Then his arms were around her. She tried to struggle, but it was only a halfhearted attempt. She gave in to him, let him bring her close. His mouth found hers in the dark and the sweetness of the kiss surprised her. When it ended, she stayed in his arms and he pulled her head down to his chest.

"If I move too fast, it's because there's so little time. I'll be leaving Bella Grande at the end of the week. I don't know when I'll be back. Come with me to New York, Angela. Come away with me."

She laughed. "You're crazy."

"You like the big city. You've told me so. We could see each other more often. We could be together, get to know all our little quirks," he said. "I could take you to Boston to meet my mother. She'd like you."

"Wait a minute!"

He leaned away from her and she could hear if not see the roguish grin on his face. "Moving too fast again?"

"Like a tornado."

His mouth sought hers again. "It's my style, honey. Can't help it. When I see what I want, I go after it and what I want right now is you."

"Want? Desire? Lusting after—is that what you mean?"

"All of that," he admitted. "Sorry if my bluntness surprises you. But I think we have something good going on, Miss Wales."

She tried to wiggle out of his arms, but he held her fast. "And I think you'd better say good night now before any more is said," she told him.

"Or done?"

"You're getting the idea," she nodded.

"Come to me then, one last minute before I go."

"I've never left, you idiot!"

"Then move in closer."

"One last kiss," she conceded.

His big hands almost circled her tiny waist. He lifted her up easily until they were on eye level.

"You know, it puts a crick in my neck every time I bend down. This is simpler—"

She wrapped her arms around him and he held her tight. His mouth found hers. Then with a laugh, he spun her around a couple of times before he set her back to the floor.

"One of these times, Angela, you're not going to close that door on me."

Then he disappeared toward his room. She heard his door slide open and close again. In a moment the lights came on, spilling out to the dark patio. Angela leaned her forehead against the cool glass and thought of the two or three walls that separated them. He was so near and yet so far and why on earth was she even thinking like this?

The next morning she joined Shawn and her father for breakfast.

"What's going on today for you?" Shawn asked.

"I think I'll start working at the hall. No one else will be wanting it, so I'll get a head start on things."

"Don't forget the party tonight," her father said.

"I'll be home in plenty of time," she replied.

Shawn's lazy gaze seemed to be devouring her and she hated the flush that rose up to her cheeks for all to see. He was smiling to himself when he lifted his coffee cup.

When they'd gone, Angela began piling things into Michael's car. The hall was used for all manner of activities on the island, but she doubted there had ever before been a one-woman photography show there. She had already picked up the key, and after driving there, she let herself in. The place was not the best for her purpose, but it would have to do. She wondered how many people would come. Notices had been sent to the Sarasota, Fort Myers, and Miami papers, but other than friends, who would really be interested? She had not reached any measure of real fame, so the general public would not care.

The day was long, hot, and troublesome. She was glad to return home, take a cool shower, and get ready for the party. Shawn and her father arrived earlier than usual.

When they all met an hour later in the living room, both men eyed her with admiration.

"Lovely, Angela. You were always a real credit to me," her father said.

"Gorgeous," Shawn said with lips pressed into a soundless whistle.

They drove in her father's rather sedate sedan, Shawn at the wheel. The dinner was at the hotel, a rambling, white frame building that had once been the epitome of grandeur on the island and now, company owned, was largely broken up into apartments such as Michael rented, and used solely for company activities.

Still there was a touch of elegance to the place and Angela had photographed it many times, always at different angles or in different light. It rose up out of the palm trees like a slumbering giant, filled with yesterday's secrets and waiting for something important to happen.

The dining room was decorated in quiet good taste. As they entered, the murmur of voices fell the moment they were seen. Then slowly, nervously, the conversations started again. Beside Angela, Shawn grew tense and reached for a cigarette. His hand trembled slightly as he lighted it.

"You're nervous! Why?" Angela asked.

"I have to make a speech," he said. "Never like to do that."

"Oh, I don't know," she said tartly. "I think you do very well in the moonlight."

His eyes turned darker as he looked intently at her for a moment. Then she gave him a smile that helped him relax. He laughed softly. "I'll settle later with you, Miss Wales."

The dinner was well prepared, typical of other such dinners, except that no one seemed relaxed. Even Edward Wales, who was always a congenial and outgoing host, had turned inward.

Then it came time for the speeches, the most boring part of the evening. Shawn spoke last on the theme of company unity. His words provoked whispers, stares, and a nervous shuffling of feet.

When the music began and people relaxed, going to the bar for drinks or grouping together in cliques as they always did, Angela was startled to look up and see Michael a few feet away.

He stood for a moment, searching the crowd for her. Then, finding her, he came toward her with quick strides.

"Angela!"

He reached out to take both of her hands tightly in his.

"Why, Michael! When did you get back?" she asked.

"Twenty minutes ago. Sorry I missed the dinner. You're a sight for sore eyes, Angela."

He leaned down and kissed her cheek. Shawn was gone from the table just then, but she saw him a few steps away, taking in the scene.

"Can you leave?" Michael asked urgently. "I want to talk with you. I need to be with you."

"I can't, Michael. I can't desert Dad. You know how it is at these parties."

Michael's disappointment was plain on his face. "I suppose you can't. Well, at least we can dance—come along, darling."

She went into his familiar arms. As he moved her around the dance floor, talking about Chicago and what he'd done and seen there, it was hard to adjust to the idea of his being back. Kelly Ross had appeared on the arm of a young man Angela didn't know. Shawn joined them. The three of them seemed to be talking in a friendly and easy way, but it seemed most of the company people were staying away from Shawn, not really mixing with him. That puzzled her. Shawn was an intelligent, likeable, bright young man. Why did they resent him so?

"You're not listening!" Michael said, annoyed. "I don't understand, Angela. Don't you care?"

She forced herself back to him with effort. "Of course I care! I'm sorry. It's just that I'm worried about things. Dad's like a stranger these days—so caught up in the company."

"It's the reorganization thing," Michael said. "Hasn't he talked to you about it?"

"No, I haven't heard anything from anyone."

They finished their dance and walked back to the table. By now Shawn was making his presence known. He reached out a hand to Michael. "You're Field, aren't you? Shawn Stevens."

Michael blinked with surprise and shook his hand. "I didn't realize you were on the island."

"Didn't Angela tell you? I'm their house guest."

Dull red crept up Michael's face. "I see."

"I believe this is our dance, Angela," Shawn said.

She couldn't refuse. Kelly said something to Michael in a low voice as they walked away. The other man had disappeared. As she moved into Shawn's arms, Angela saw Michael and Kelly talking together.

"Why didn't you tell him about me?" Shawn asked.

"No reason."

"He doesn't like sharing you, does he?"

"I don't want to talk about Michael."

"Did he say anything about transferring off the island?"

"No, and that surprised me. Probably later."

"I fixed it," he said. "At least for the moment."

"What?"

"He'll be staying on Bella Grande for another couple of months anyway. I hope that makes you happy."

She hardly knew what to say. "How did you manage that?"

He lifted his shoulders in a shrug. "I know a few people in the right places. I thought you'd be pleased."

"I'm stunned. But I thank you for Michael's sake."

His arm tightened ever so slightly around her. "And what about you?"

"I'm happy for him."

"Is that all?" he asked, amusement tugging at the corners of his mouth.

"I hate that arrogant look you give me."

He laughed. "Darling, you might as well face a few facts. I've always found it's best. You belong to me. No one else."

The music stopped at that precise moment. She turned on her heel to walk back to Michael. When she reached the table, she found him with an angry flush on his face. By the same token, Kelly had leaned away with a frigid smile on her lips. Angela looked from one to the other.

"What's going on?"

"I think I'd better find Pete," Kelly said quickly. "Excuse me."

She was gone in an instant. Michael refused to talk about it. In a moment, Shawn murmured his excuses and left them alone.

"Someday your friend Kelly is going to go too far," Michael said.

"Want to tell me about it?"

He turned his gaze toward her and shook his head. "It's not important, darling. Only you are important."

He leaned toward her. Normally Michael was not demonstrative in public. Nor was Angela, although she had no qualms about it as he did. But out of the corner of her eye, she saw Shawn watching them covertly. She wrapped her arms around Michael's neck and kissed him very soundly and thoroughly.

He was pleased, if embarrassed. "You did miss me!" he said happily.

"More than you know," she said.

The party broke up about midnight. Michael left earlier than that, saying he had a report he had to do before going to work the next day. Shawn and her father were the last to leave and Angela waited for them in the car. She heard them talking together as they walked toward her.

"You didn't tell them, Shawn," her father said.

"Another few days won't hurt. No use in stirring them up more than needed."

"Still—"

"Wait," Shawn said with an air of authority. "We'll wait."

At Casa Linda, they offered Angela a nightcap, but she shook her head, said good night, and disappeared into her room. Nevertheless, she could not sleep. All sorts of thoughts raced through her head. Her show, Michael, Shawn, lying in the sand beside him, being lifted up in his arms, being kissed so completely. She returned to the present with a sigh. Shawn would soon be gone. Perhaps then her life would be normal, and she could concentrate more completely on her work. She could find what she wanted somewhere. But what exactly did she want? The need was always there, in the depths of her soul, just beyond reach, hiding in the shadows . . .

She was awakened by Kelly Ross, who came bouncing into the room in a pair of bright-colored shorts and huge sunglasses perched upon her short nose.

"Get up, sleepyhead. Today's the picnic, remember?"

"Oh, Kelly, do I have to go?" she asked with a sleepy yawn.

"A promise is a promise. Out with you."

Angela was stunned to see that it was so late.

"Why didn't Emma call me?"

"She's gone to do the marketing, I suppose. No one's here. I let myself in."

With Kelly prodding, Angela quickly dressed and gulped down the instant coffee Kelly made. Going out to Kelly's convertible, she saw that it was a perfect day for a picnic.

"Where is this feast being held?" she asked.

"Down at the far end, near the airstrip. The bus will soon be ready to leave. We'll follow it."

"I wonder how I managed to let you talk me into this."

"Relax and enjoy," Kelly said. "It seems to me you've been keyed up these last few days."

"Reasons," Angela said with another yawn.

"First thing—you'd better have a dip in the Gulf to wake up."

Angela braced herself for the day. She was amazed at the amount of noise seventeen ten-year-olds could produce. There was never so much frolicking, so much shouting, so much screeching laughter as there was that day. Surprisingly Angela found that she was enjoying herself. For one thing, Thomasita was one of the children. She was always a favorite, and Angela held a long conversation with her on an assortment of topics, such as why butterflies fly, how whiskey is made, and where sea gulls go at night. Angela shot still more film and knew that she had probably gotten some good shots.

"See, the day isn't a total loss," Kelly said.

"I'm having fun. When do we eat? I'm starving."

The picnic food, provided by the children's mothers, was spread out on tablecloths over the sand. Food had never tasted better than on a day like this, and once everyone had eaten their fill, the children became quieter. Some flew kites, others built sand castles, and one or two crept away for a nap under the shade of the palm trees. Angela sought such a place herself.

She drifted with the clouds. A tanker steamed toward the docks with a load of oil. A fishing boat chugged along on the horizon. Harvey Davis's yacht skimmed by with Brenda at the wheel. Everything seemed to blend with the hot summer day. Sand shimmered in the sunlight, and the surf receded and flowed back, bringing foam, new shells, and fresh sand.

Angela dropped off into a world of brilliant colors. She dreamed of Shawn, saw his bronzed shoulders and a tiny white scar on his chest. She touched the black of his hair, drowned in the gold specks of his hazel eyes. He wore red swimming trunks and he lifted her into his arms and began carrying her away. Farther and farther they went, and just when she thought she might see where he was taking her, she woke up.

"What is it?" Kelly asked.

She had stretched out beside Angela on a beach towel, her nose covered with suntan oil.

"I was dreaming."

"So?"

"In color. Not everyone dreams in color, you know. And this was so vivid."

"Must have been a nice dream. You were smiling."

Angela shielded her eyes from the sun. "Strange—I didn't know he had a white scar there."

"You're not making any sense, you know," Kelly grinned. "And I think it's time we began gathering everyone up. End of the last day of school. It's been a nice one."

"Could you drop me off at the hall on the way back?" Angela asked.

"Sure."

After the hot sun of the beach and the blinding sunlight, Angela found the community hall delightfully cool and shadowy. She had set up enough easels to hold her major photos, the ones she thought should take priority. The others were to be hung on the walls. She had already brought some of the photos and she began experimenting with the right spot for them.

With a mouth full of tacks and a small hammer, she began nailing them to the wall, stepping back now and then to study them as objectively as possible.

She didn't hear his steps, but suddenly she knew he was in the room with her.

"I wish you wouldn't do that," she said.

Shawn grinned. "You were so absorbed in your work, I didn't want to disturb you. And such work! I've been looking at all of this, Angela."

"Still more to come," she said.

Naturally he honed in on the photos of Banner Oil. The tanks, despite their ugliness, could be made to look very interesting and she had tried for a different effect.

From those he went to the pictures she had taken around the island—of the yacht club, the fishing boats, and the airstrip. Finally he came to her studies of José. He lingered for a long time, gazing into José's weathered face and seasoned eyes.

64

"José," he said. "This has to be José."

"Yes."

"What a man! Such character in that face. I want to meet him. Could you arrange it?"

"Probably."

"You seem surprised."

"Maybe there's red blood flowing in your veins after all, instead of just oil," she said with a wicked thrust.

"You know there is."

He moved on, taking his time, and she found herself anxious for any remark he made. He lingered for a long while at pictures of the Casa Linda, the sea forming a backdrop.

"Lovely," he said. "Absolutely lovely, Angela. How did *Top Fashion Magazine* ever let you escape them?"

"It wasn't hard, Darling," she said.

"Shame. Darling, you have to do something about this. I hope some important people see all this great work."

"I hope so, too," she said. "But who knows? It's a tough world out there."

He laughed and agreed. "But you're special, Angela. I think the world will hear from you all right."

"I'm glad you like what I do."

"Very much."

She didn't doubt him. He was sincere. Then his seriousness was shattered by a roguish grin. "But I don't see any pinups here. Don't you dig young, husky men?"

"Want to pose?" she shot back.

He turned to her quickly, eyes flashing. "Any time."

"Sorry. That's not my cup of tea."

Then suddenly she remembered her strange, technicolored dream. She peered at his chest, wishing she could see through the cloth of his shirt and the lapel of his summer jacket. But of course he didn't have a little white scar. That had only been a dream.

"You've caught the island, Angela, in every possible way. With its Sunday face on and with its hair down. But there's one angle you don't have."

"Can't be," she argued. "I defy you to tell me how else I could have shot pictures of the island."

"Want to bet a kiss or two?"

"You're on," she said quickly. "And you've already lost—"

He shook his head slowly. "Sorry, honey, but you lose. From the air, from a plane—no aerial shots."

She flushed. He was right!

"So, I'll take you up one day soon. It will be a date when I come back to Bella Grande."

"I could get some super shots, couldn't I?"

"I believe you owe me a debt," he said quietly.

He reached out for her. "It will have to last me until I get back. I'm flying out tonight."

"Oh!"

Then he bent his head and his kiss took away everything else, her breath, her sight, her strength.

When he let her go, he smiled at her. "Soon, darling— I'll come back to you soon."

Chapter V

It was D-day. At least the skies were clear and the sun was bright. Angela lay in bed for a long time thinking about the one-woman show she was going to present that afternoon and evening. The hall was ready. The photos, changed at least three different times the day before, were waiting for public viewing. As she had stood looking at her work the previous day, she had thought of how much of her life was wrapped up in the photos. Some had been taken long ago when she had first begun experimenting with film at fifteen. Still, some of those early photographs were surprisingly good. There was a raw eagerness to them that perhaps she no longer had. Now she was polished and controlled.

Kelly was coming by for breakfast to help with any last-minute details and help calm Angela's butterflies.

"You really surprise me, you know," Kelly said when she arrived. "I thought you'd take all of this in stride and yet you're as excited as a little kid!"

"Nervous," she admitted. "It's like laying your heart out on the chopping block for everyone to see."

"Maybe we should call a spade a spade and admit to what is really bothering you," Kelly said. "Have you heard from Phillip?"

Angela shook her head. "I doubt it. No, I don't expect

him or anyone else from New York. Once you leave, you're forgotten."

Kelly poured her a cup of coffee. "Better drink this. It's going to be a long day."

Edward Wales was out on the patio, his breakfast eaten long ago, and he came in with an encouraging word and a pat on the shoulder. "It will go just great, dear. Wait and see."

"Will you come early or late?"

"I'm coming early before the crowd gathers. It's been a while since I've had a good look at your work, Angela."

It was true. While she had demanded his attention a few times in the past, most of the time she let him alone. He was always busy in his own tight little world.

They arrived at the hall after an early lunch. Satisfied that she had done the best she could with what she had, Angela began to pace about, waiting for the first visitor. It turned out to be Michael.

With him came a large bouquet of roses, which Kelly whisked away to put in a vase. Then, tugging her along with him, Michael took the grand tour, pausing for a moment at each photo. Her spirits began to lift. Michael had always been a good judge of her work and he put honesty before everything. He was pleased with what he saw.

Soon others came. Most of them were Banner Oil people or old friends from the island. Angela kept watching for José, but by late afternoon he had not arrived.

"Aren't you going to take a break for something to eat?" Kelly asked. "I'll stay here."

"No, I don't want to leave."

José chose a time when he knew no one else would be there. He came in his Sunday suit with a string tie and highly polished shoes. Thomasita clung to his hand, her black hair tied back with a bright ribbon. Angela went to greet them.

"I was getting worried you wouldn't come," she said.

"I wouldn't have missed it, Angela," José said. "It's time I saw what you do with those cameras of yours."

He looked at the pictures of the island without saying a word, but shook his head and murmured to himself.

"That means he likes them, Angela," Thomasita whispered.

Angela was conscious of holding her breath as he neared the huge photograph of himself. He seemed almost stunned when he stared at it. Then he grinned, slowly at first and then broadly.

"By golly, Angela, it's pretty good."

She laughed, delighted. "I'm glad you're pleased."

"You make music with your camera, Angela. That's what you do."

She kissed his brown cheek. "That's all the praise I need today," she said warmly.

Soon they had gone and no one else came. Angela experienced a letdown. Phillip was not coming. Up until now she had been watching for him, one little corner of her heart refusing to admit that he had really and truly put her out of his life.

One pleasant surprise came in the form of an art critic who had a column in a Miami paper. He came in like a cool breeze, studied her work, asked a few questions, took a photograph or two, and disappeared.

"I really wowed him, didn't I?" Angela asked wryly.

"Probably did," Kelly said. "You can never tell about those people."

They planned to close the hall at eight. Michael was expected back to help her pack her work and take it back to Casa Linda, but Angela decided to wait until the next day. She suddenly couldn't bear even to look at the photos anymore. Michael, who had arrived a few minutes earlier, suggested that they go out somewhere.

"You've had a long day of it, Angela."

"No, thanks. I think I just want to go home and be alone—"

"You're sure?"

"Yes."

He nodded, his gentle eyes filled with understanding. "Okay, I'll call you first thing in the morning. Shall we have Sunday brunch at the club before we collect your things here?"

"Call me," she said wearily. "We'll see."

She sent both Michael and Kelly away a few minutes before eight. No one else was going to come. She had begun to put out the lights when she heard a familiar footstep. She would have known the sound of that hard footfall anywhere. She turned around slowly, fearful that her imagination was playing tricks.

Phillip Blazer was not as tall as Shawn or Michael. He was almost stockily built, but there was a vitality about him that made women look twice. His hair was a rusty blond. He had quick blue eyes, a hard chin, a full mouth, and, if not Hollywood handsome, he was not far from it.

"Hello, Angela."

"I didn't think you'd come!"

He strode into the room, hands in his pockets. "I should have phoned, but I wanted to surprise you. There were delays at the Atlanta airport where I changed planes. Sorry—looks as if I almost missed the show."

They looked carefully at each other, assessing one another. He looked a trifle older, but perhaps it was only fatigue and exasperation at the delay. He hated to be late for anything and lost his temper over schedules that went awry. But his smile was the same, his eyes still flashed, and his vital sex appeal came beaming toward her as clear and sharp as ever.

"You look lovely as always, Angela," he said.

"Thank you."

"It seems a long time."

"It has been," she agreed. "I hope you can stay a few days. You'll like Bella Grande once you have the grand tour."

"Not much time. I have a late plane to catch. About midnight. But there's time for me to review your show. Then I'd like to talk with you, Angela. Is there a place we can go?"

"Yes."

He reached out his hand to her. "Come now. Show me your work."

She flipped on the lights, and walking with her hand under his arm, his warm fingers covering hers, they strode along together. When he asked questions, she gave him all the technical answers he wanted to hear, the speed of the film she had used, the type, the lens, the aperture setting, and how she had strived for certain effects.

He moved slowly, saying nothing. He would wait until he had seen it all, then he would tell her in detail what was wrong and why. She both dreaded and longed to hear what he would say.

"I can't believe you're here," she said.

"I can't either," he admitted, looking at her for a long moment. "We parted company on rather bad terms. I thought I never wanted to see you again, Angela. Then when Janice Holt told me about this—I found I couldn't pass it up. It was an easy way to come back into your life."

Her heart began knocking at the thought of this possibility. "Is that why you've come?"

"We'll talk later," he said. Then, pressing a finger to his lips for silence, they walked on. She tried to read his face for opinions and thoughts, but it was impossible to do. The last picture she showed him was the one of José. He looked at it the longest and then smiled at her.

"It has all your warmth, Angela. It has to be your best. This lighting—how did you get such an effect?"

She laughed and shook her head. "Trade secret."

He made a face, one that she remembered seeing many times when she was working for him on the magazine. It meant that he understood, but didn't like to be kept in the dark. Phillip wanted his finger in every pie. Maybe that was what had made him such a good editor. The magazine was his baby in every sense of the word and it never had colic or needed changing or broke out with the measles unless he knew it.

"What about the others?" she asked.

"I'll tell you over a drink. Can we leave now?"

"Yes."

She turned out the lights, locked the door, and together they walked out into the warm night. Phillip had rented a car at the mainland airport and she directed him to the yacht club. Saturday nights were traditionally the busiest there, but there was a small booth in the lounge and they took it. Nestled in the deep leather with a tiny table between them, knees nearly touching, they regarded each other in the dim light.

"Seems like old times. This is a nice place," Phillip said.

"All New Yorkers expect a Podunk sort of place. Bella Grande lives up to its Spanish name—beautiful and grand."

Phillip smiled at her and reached out to touch her hand. She sat very still, waiting. She had imagined this moment many times, but she had not expected it to come here in the bar of the yacht club, with a Saturday-night crowd all around.

"You want to know about your show—I can say it in one word, Angela. Smashing!"

She closed her eyes and heaved a deep sigh of relief.

"I'm glad to see you have put your time to good use here, Angela. I think it's time you needed. You've sharpened your perspective. Your talent has grown. There's a new awareness to your work. I'm impressed."

"Thank you."

"I hope it means something, coming from me," he said quietly.

"I never questioned your judgment in such matters," she said.

He lifted his lips. "We worked well together, didn't we? Until personal issues got in the way."

She felt her insides tighten. She felt this awful, wretched way every time she thought about Phillip in that other woman's arms and how blithely blind she had been to it all. How naive she had been about a man like Phillip. There had been innuendos around the office, whispers among the women about what a ladies' man he was, but she had not heeded them. She had gone into it wide-eyed, open-hearted, crazy-in-love.

"What are your plans now?" he asked. "With the show behind you? I know it was something you always wanted to do so that's one goal reached."

"I'm hoping there will be some repercussions—some interest. But with only one art critic showing up . . ." She laughed shortly. "I think my holiday is nearly over. I'll be out looking for some place that can use my work."

Phillip was toying with his lighter. He snapped it on and off a few times and looked at her for a moment with a veiled expression on his face.

"I've been doing a little string-pulling, Angela. I think I can manage it now if you're interested. How would you like to come back to New York and work with me again?"

Joy shot through her and then she leaned back, remembering that she must be cautious this time.

"But I understand that photographers like me are a dime a dozen in the city."

He flushed, remembering that those had been his exact words to her. "I had that coming."

"Yes, you did," she said evenly.

"You still have that ribbon of steel in you, haven't you?" he said. "Well, that's okay. You need it to survive these days. But you didn't answer me."

"I couldn't answer tonight," she said. "I'd have to think about it."

"I can't wait very long," he said pointedly.

She felt excitement weaving through her bones, crying out for her to answer yes. She had loved New York. While photographing top models wearing high-fashion designer clothes had been a chore at times, there had been other compensations—the city itself, which could be a photographer's paradise; the feeling of being in the swing of things; and, of course, there had been Phillip.

He gave her his handsome smile and lifted his glass to her. "To you, darling. I know you'll make the right decision."

"And just where do you fit into the picture, Phillip?"

He lowered his glass. His eyes were too bright, too quick. "Wherever you want me, darling."

She wanted to believe that and trust it. But could she?

"We had some good times, Angela. Really good times."

"Yes."

"We could again."

Then he leaned across the table and kissed her lightly on the lips. It was the exactly right tantalizing touch—something she should have expected from him. It left her wanting more.

He looked at his watch with an air of impatience. "Damn! I have to leave if I'm to catch that plane—want to come with me—now?"

She laughed. "No."

"When will you call?"

"Soon."

"Promise?"

"I never break a promise," she said. "I won't break this one. But I have to ask about Deloris."

He drained his glass and put it aside. His smile was noncommittal.

"Deloris? Finished. Long ago. I told you it wasn't serious, but you wouldn't listen."

"Why have you waited so long to tell me?"

"I'm not the sort that rakes over cold ashes looking for a new spark. So for me to break the pattern, it must mean, darling, that you're more important to me than you know."

They went back to the car. Walking with Phillip Angela felt alive and happy. He was easily the most exciting man she knew. He brought out the best in her—or did he? She hadn't done so badly since being on Bella Grande.

He left her quickly, without saying another word. It was his way. She watched him drive away and wondered what he was thinking, if he was smiling, or if he was frowning with uncertainty. But when had Phillip Blazer been uncertain about anything?

With the show behind her, Angela soon felt at loose ends—and there was Phillip's tempting offer. Dare she take that step back? Could she risk heartache again?

Kelly guessed at once what was up. Sunday, after the show, Michael decided he could not spend the day with her because of some unfinished reports due at his office on Monday morning. Kelly suggested a game of tennis at the school tennis courts.

"It will help you unwind, Angela."

"All right."

Smashing the tennis ball with all her vim and vigor, chasing to the net and then backing away to the sidelines, Kelly kept her hopping. She was expert at the game and it wasn't long before she had whipped Angela soundly.

"I should know better," Angela laughed, gasping for breath.

"Enough?"

"Yes!" Angela nodded. "Let's go home and find something cool to drink."

Over chilled glasses of iced tea with lemon Kelly put it to her point blank.

"Is it on with Phillip again?"

"It could be," Angela sighed, "if I want it to be. I don't know, Kelly. I've never been on such a hot tin roof before. Which way do I jump?"

Kelly sipped her tea and gave Angela a winsome smile. "Where does Michael enter into all of this?"

Angela put her head back and closed her eyes. "I don't know. I truly don't know."

"It seems he's often the forgotten party in your life," Kelly said.

There was an edge in her voice. Angela heard it, but ignored it. They had exchanged heated words more than once about Michael Field. Once she had questioned Kelly about her defense of him.

"It's the schoolteacher in me, I suppose. I want things to be right."

"Maybe I should go to New York, look around, get the feel of the place again," Angela said. "That might help me decide. Hey, want to come with me?"

Kelly considered it for a moment and shook her head. "I'm taking some summer courses at the college on the mainland to add to my teaching credits. Couldn't make it."

"Nuts!"

Kelly grinned. "You don't need me anyway, Angela. You've always been so darned independent."

"I think I'll drift for a few days. Be lazy. I'll decide later."

They let the rest of the afternoon dwindle away, and, after Kelly had gone, Angela ate a quiet dinner with her father. He seemed so preoccupied these days. She asked him about it.

"Oh, just business," he laughed. "And I'm sorry I bring it home with me so much."

"I wish you wouldn't let it worry you so."

He didn't deny that it did.

Faced with a long evening, Angela was surprised and pleased when Michael came by and took her away.

"Let's get off this blasted island," he said.

He drove steadily through the residential area of Bella Grande, crossed the causeway, tossed coins into the toll box, and rolled on.

"You haven't told me about Phillip Blazer," he said.

"How did you know . . ."

"Does it matter?" Michael's jaw was hard and set. "What did it mean? Phillip's coming here?"

"He came to see my work."

Michael laughed shortly. "Oh, sure!"

"If you must know, he offered me my old job back."

Michael gripped the steering wheel. "And are you going?"

"I really don't want to talk about it, Michael. It seems everything is up in the air."

"Well, at least my work has stabilized. I don't know for how long. It's a crazy company. One day they say they'll do one thing, the next—who knows! I don't want you to leave, Angela, now that I'll still be here."

Michael reached out and squeezed her hand. "I love you, Angela. You're so free and sweet and you make my head spin! I'm never sure I'm going to be able to handle you."

"No man handles me," she retorted.

Michael's blue eyes twinkled at that. "But it's a lot of fun trying."

They spent a pleasant evening doing very little. With Michael it seemed the simple things in life were the best. With Phillip life had been hectic, rushing to concerts, dinners, or shows, not to mention innumerable cocktail parties, many of which seemed to last forever. Phillip knew so many people, opened so many doors for her, took her along in a heady rush of life.

It was late when Michael finally saw Angela home. At the door of Casa Linda, he kissed her for a long, sweet moment.

When he had gone and she watched him drive away, it occurred to her how simple everything would be if she just fell madly in love with him. She was fond of him, perhaps even loved him a little, but it was not the heady experience she wanted. Phillip had given her a taste of what it should be. And at the thought of Shawn she found herself covered with gooseflesh. He was off the island but not off her mind.

She slept restlessly, got up once to stare out at the night, and thought of walking on the beach, but gave up the idea. Instead, she settled for a glass of milk and a novel.

She fell asleep at last, and awakened to find the sun in her eyes. Her father had gone more than an hour before. In the kitchen Emma put a cup of coffee in front of her and shook her head.

"You were up prowling half the night."

"Sorry if I awakened you."

"What's wrong, Angela?"

She looked into Emma's kind, motherly face and shook her head. "I wish I knew."

"Oh, dear! When you begin talking like that, I know that you're getting far too restless and the next thing I know you'll be packing up and moving on."

"Maybe," she admitted.

"Why don't you go and see your Aunt Franny?" she asked. "Tennessee would be cool and green this time of year. You love the Smoky Mountains."

She considered the idea and quickly discarded it. She loved her aunt, but a visit would mean making polite conversation, visiting with her friends, and being shown off in a way that she didn't want right now.

The phone rang and Angela went to answer it. Michael's voice sounded happy and pleased.

"Have you read the Miami paper this morning?"

"No."

"Better look!"

"You mean they reviewed the show?"

"You'd better believe it!"

He hung up and she rushed to find the paper. Her father had not taken time to open it, and it still lay on the dining-room table. With frantic hands she thumbed through it until she found the right section. The write-up was brief, not at all flowery, but the last line thrilled her: "Miss Wales is a woman to watch, a photographer of some worth."

Emma reached for it with a pleased smile. "That's very nice, Angela."

"It's not very much," Angela admitted, "but enough to spur me on. I think I'll go for a walk."

Emma was laughing as Angela went to find her camera. What was there left on Bella Grande for her to shoot? She remembered Shawn's promise to take her up in his plane. Aerial shots would be a challenge, but one she was ready to meet.

She wandered down to José's cottage. He was mending a torn net and she watched his gnarled hands working nimbly in a craft only a few had mastered as well.

"So?" José asked.

She told him about the news item and he nodded. "Good."

"The trouble is, José, I don't know what to do next. Do you ever feel like that?"

He grinned. "Never had that luxury. It was always go out and get the fish. If it was raining or storming, it meant stay in, make boat repairs, mend nets, build new traps."

"You make it sound more simple than it was," she frowned.

"How so?"

"You had a wife, raised a son, now have a granddaughter. It had to be more than that."

"What weighs you down today, *poca minina*?"

She tossed her small hands in the air. "Everything!"

"That's *mucho*," he said.

For a while she romped with Thomasita on the beach and finally went home, realizing she had not taken one picture.

Dinner was late. Her father was delayed and when he came it was nearly sundown. He ate hurriedly, saying he had work to do in the study. Angela started to protest, but Emma gave her a look and she decided to say nothing.

It was some time after dinner that she heard the doorbell. Emma answered it and in a moment she heard footsteps going down the hall. Someone to see Dad. She stepped out of her bedroom to the patio and thought of a swim. A light suddenly came on in the guest room and she stared with surprise. In a moment Shawn stepped out through the sliding glass doors. He lit a cigarette and in the flame of his lighter she saw his face for one brief moment. He looked tired. A line was cut deeply in his forehead between his eyes.

Then he sensed her presence and looked through the darkness for her.

"Hello," he said.

"You're back!"

"Sooner than I expected," he nodded. "Your father graciously told me to come here whenever I needed a room—so, here I am."

She felt a smothered excitement at the thought of him in the house again.

"There are rooms at the old hotel—especially for Banner people."

"I'm aware of that," he said.

He strode toward her. He had shed his jacket and tie and loosened his collar. His sleeves were rolled up midway to his elbows and Angela remembered his masculinity, his strong arms, and his exciting hands. For the first time since her show, she felt alive again.

"How did it go Saturday?" he asked.

He was very close now. She could feel his gaze devouring her.

"It went better than I expected."

"I saw the Miami paper today," he said. "I was impressed and very proud."

"Thank you."

He laughed and the sound of it went rippling across her mind like the tide coming in over white sand, churning up all sorts of ideas and thoughts.

"I've missed this place," he said.

"You've only been gone three days," she pointed out.

He reached out and wrapped a lock of her hair around the end of his finger. "You've been counting."

"What brings you back?"

"Many things. I didn't think I'd be here quite this soon, but I'm glad. Anything to see you again, Angela."

His hand slid under her hair and crept along the back of her neck, caressing her. "You haven't greeted me properly."

He bent his head forward. She told herself not to let this happen, not to start up this dizzy relationship again. But she couldn't move. He held her fast and his mouth came down with fresh hunger, new desire.

"You've missed me," he said with an air of satisfaction.

"Don't put words in my mouth," she answered as tartly as she could.

His grin, roguish and touched by the devil, told her that he knew he was right.

"We'd be foolish not to admit what's happening, Angela. There's a sweet fire between us whenever we meet. I for one don't want to put it out. I want to see just how high it's going to burn."

"I told you never to count on me. I may be leaving the island very soon."

"Not yet," he said, shaking his head. "We've too much unfinished business."

"Such as?"

"A plane ride over the island—as many rides as you want to do your work. Then we've got a lot of talking to do, about a great many things."

"What really brought you back to Bella Grande?"

He let his hand drop away and for a moment he stiffened and seemed angry. "Did your father tell you to ask that?"

"Don't be silly! He never talks about confidential matters and I assume what you're doing here is somehow secret."

"It won't be after tomorrow. I don't relish tomorrow. I wish it were over."

He wouldn't tell her any more and right then, sensing there was something almost ominous afoot, she didn't want to hear.

"Let's go for a swim. Not in the pool—in the Gulf."

"Only idiots go out at night."

"I suppose you're right. But we'd be together."

She was tempted. The Gulf at night was as enchanting as in the bright sunlight, perhaps more so. There was something special and unique about swimming anywhere in the dark.

"I don't think so, Shawn. I think you'd better just say good night."

He tossed his cigarette away. "Tomorrow night?"

"I never count on tomorrow. I never plan that far ahead."

"One thing you can count on," he said firmly, "is me. I'm going swimming with you—tomorrow night!"

Then, as he had before, he lifted her off the ground with his large, strong hands until she was eye level with him.

"Say good night, darling."

She wished there was enough light to see his eyes. But she didn't need to see. She could sense the desire in them, the dark glow of golden specks in the clear hazel. She could almost see the outline of his mouth. It was not hard to find his lips in the dark, nor to answer their swift, urgent passion. She broke away with effort.

"Put me down."

"Someday," he sighed. "Someday."

He let her go and she felt the solid ground under her feet again. She managed to reach her room, to close the glass doors. He stood just beyond them, watching her. Her hand was trembling as she pulled the drapes and turned on the light, shutting him out.

Chapter VI

Angela had just finished developing a roll of film in the darkroom when Emma pounded at her door.

"Can you come out?"

"In a second," Angela called back.

When she opened the door, she found Emma standing with her father's briefcase.

"Your father forgot this and he just phoned. He wonders if you could bring it to the office."

"Okay."

It had been some time since she had visited the offices of Banner Oil. When she had been young and the apple of her father's eye, he had taken her to show her off to his fellow employees. But she was past that now and she preferred keeping her life separate from that place. It wasn't that she hated the oil company. It was the livelihood of most of the people on the island and it was her father's life, but she did resent it at times. People sometimes forgot that there was an outside world.

She drove in her bright red car with the top down. The sun slid warmly along her arms and she could feel the sea breeze against her face. The guard at the gate recognized her and allowed her to drive through. She parked her car and hurried inside the cool, concrete-block building.

She went straight toward her father's office and met

Harvey Davis on the way. He looked cross and when he saw her, his lips curled in a scornful smile.

"Well, well, if it isn't Shawn Stevens's little playmate."

Angela flushed. "What's wrong with you, Harvey?"

"If you think buttering up to Stevens is going to save your father's job, you'd better think twice."

She was puzzled by his behavior. "Harvey, you're not supposed to drink on company time."

He muttered something as she hurried away, brushing his antagonism aside. Harvey always shot off his mouth about nothing.

Angela left the briefcase with her father's secretary. He was busy on the phone, so she didn't go in to say hello, but Shawn Stevens arrived just then and gave her a pleased look.

"Well, what a nice surprise. I missed you at breakfast," he said.

"I overslept," she answered with a shrug.

She knew that the secretary wasn't missing a word. She also realized that the conversation could take on another light if not clarified.

"What time did you leave the house with Dad?" she asked. "And was the guest room comfortable?"

"Eight to the first question, and yes, it was very comfortable," he said.

He quirked a dark brow at her. She gave him a polite smile. "Good-bye now, I must run."

He let her get halfway down the hall before he called to her. He strode toward her with a grin.

"That was quite a little performance in there," he said.

"People talk," she replied. "And I suspect there is considerable talk about you already without adding fuel to the fire."

"Listen, I was just going out to inspect the tanks—a hard-hat job. Would you like to come along?"

"Will I pass security?"

"If you're with me. Come along, darling."

"Don't call me that!" she hissed.

"Why not? I call you that other times—like last night. By the way, it was the kind of welcome home that I like!"

She flushed as he took her arm and propelled her down the hall. They stopped in an office he was using, where he snatched up two yellow hard hats. Tucking them under his arm, they walked out to one of the company cars.

"Why are you inspecting the tanks? That can't be your job. I thought you were some kind of executive."

He nodded. "I am. But I'm also under orders to give a full report about everything—that includes the depots. It was a job I wasn't looking forward to, but now, with you—it might even be fun."

The offices were located a short distance from the supply depot, and once through the security gate, Shawn drove up and down the lane between each tank, stopping now and then to make notes on a clipboard.

Sometimes he climbed the winding steps up the side of the tank to the very top. She watched him up there, prancing around as if he were only two feet from the ground.

"I wish you didn't have to do that," she told him when he climbed into the car.

"Afraid of heights?" he asked.

"No, but it looks so dangerous."

A thoughtful look had been deepening on his face. "I'm not too happy with some of the things I've seen. Everything is getting out of date. The equipment is old. We really need to do something about some of this."

"Oh, I've heard that old song before. Dad's been yelling his head off for a long time now."

Shawn scowled. "Yes, I know."

"And by the way, did you chew on Harvey this morning?"

Shawn gave her a quick, hard look. "Davis?"

"Yes."

"Why do you ask?"

"He said some very peculiar things to me when I met him in the hall," Angela said. "Now that I think about it, it was something about my father—"

Shawn cut in. "Listen, I've seen all I need to see here right now and it's only an hour until lunchtime. We didn't have that swim last night—why not do it now."

"Now!"

He grinned. "I don't often goof off. Truth is, things need to simmer down at the office. I think everyone would be happier if they didn't see me for a little while. How about it—the water's calm, the sun is warm, the sand is waiting."

"I thought we were doing that tonight."

He shook his head. "Tonight we're going up in the plane. Have your camera loaded—I'm going to give you a thrill or two."

"If you're one of those crazy stunt flyers . . ."

"I have been in my heyday. But I'll behave tonight, I promise."

She looked out to the Gulf, inviting as always, and Shawn kept pressing until the next thing she knew she had agreed. They returned to Casa Linda, changed into swimming clothes, and then drove to a particularly quiet place she knew. Her secret little cove was not far away, for this stretch of beach was her favorite.

Leaving their beach towels and sunglasses under a palm tree, Shawn caught her hand in his and with a laugh they began running toward the waiting water. They splashed in and she felt the tug of the surf stirring the sand under her feet. She began to swim and Shawn swam beside her, his long brown arms stroking the water easily, powerfully. They had gone out only a few feet in the clear, azure water when Angela laughed and pointed.

"Our friends," she said.

"You're sure?" he asked.

"No sharks here," she assured him. "They're porpoises. They like people, you know."

She always marveled at the big fish, leaping as they swam, playing with each other. There was a school of them, and they were heading north.

"How free and easy they are!" Shawn said with delight.

"I love to watch them."

"They're almost out of sight now," he said.

"And we've come too far from shore. We must go back."

"Agreed," he said.

It was fun swimming beside him. They paced themselves with steady, sure strokes and soon the beach was very near. He gave her a shout. "Race you in! Last one there has to buy lunch!"

He beat her by two strokes. He was waiting for her with his hand outstretched as she waded out.

"You lose," he said.

"I never agreed to the bet!"

He walked away, pulling her along to the cool shade of the palm tree. There they wiped away the salt water with their towels and Shawn spread a couple of dry ones on the sand.

"What a sky! I may never go back to work."

He stretched out, his hands under his head, and asked her to light a cigarette for him.

"Lazy!"

"I won't deny it," he sighed. "What a day."

She found his cigarettes and lit one for him. He took it from her hand, his eyes giving her a long, caressing look.

"Thanks, darling."

"I thought you were going to stop smoking."

He grinned. "I will—I promise. The day I feel I have everything I want out of life, I'll quit."

"Some promise!" she said wryly.

She started to put his cigarettes away when she saw the tiny little white scar on his chest, exactly where she had dreamed it had been. She felt a little stunned.

"What's wrong?" he asked.

She traced the scar with a fingertip. "Where did you get that?"

"A slight accident when I was a boy. I fell through a window. Lucky I wasn't cut worse than that. Funny you should notice, it's so tiny."

She felt a strange buzzing in her head. Good heavens! Maybe it was supposed to happen like this. She had never believed in fate, at least not like this! There had to be a logical explanation for knowing that the scar was there.

"I've never seen you without your shirt before, have I?"

"Not unless you tiptoed into my room one night and I didn't know it," he teased. "What's so important about a little scar?"

She couldn't tell him she had dreamed about it, so she passed it off with a shrug. "Nothing."

"Come here," he said. "Lie down beside me and watch the sky. It's putting on a great show for us today."

The clouds were clumped into thick wads of white and Shawn looked for pictures in them.

"A poodle over there. See him?"

"Yes. And an old man smoking a pipe over there."

"And there's a bunch of grapes. And a rocket."

"Did you do this when you were a boy?"

"Constantly. I was a terrible daydreamer. I used to wander off in Indiana for a day at a time. There was a woods near where we lived. I used to go there, tramp around, find a nice quiet spot, lie down like this, and dream."

"About what?"

"You."

"What!"

He laughed. "The perfect woman. What I'd do when I found her and what I'd say and then I'd be afraid I'd make a horrible mess of it."

"I can't imagine your ever thinking you were shy," she said caustically.

"Don't you know my cockiness is just a disguise? It's to hide the fact that I'm scared to death of a pretty woman like you."

"Baloney," she retorted.

He grinned and put his hand on her hair, stroking it, fingering it as if inspecting a piece of fine silk.

"What did you dream about when you were a girl?"

"Winning every prize there was for photography."

He groaned. "Lord, woman, do you ever think of anything else?"

"I'm dedicated."

"You're obsessed! What about love, home, kids . . ."

"I want them all, in due time."

"You make it sound like something that's going to be spit out from a computer."

"Everything to its season," she replied with a sigh. "I'm sleepy. The water, the sun . . ."

"Go to sleep on me," he threatened, "and I'll pick you up and toss you into the Gulf!"

"You wouldn't."

"Try me," he said.

"It's probably best to keep my eyes open," she decided.

"That's better."

"At least it's smarter."

"Your father has worked on Bella Grande for the last twenty-two years. Before that—"

"I don't remember much about it, but we lived in Louisiana—in the New Orleans area."

"Ah, yes. Now and then I hear a touch of the South in your voice."

"You're imagining it!"

He leaned on his elbow and looked at her. "I have an ear for such things. You're a southern belle in disguise."

"My, my, you certainly are an expert at many things, aren't you?"

His eyes lighted with mischief. "I can hear your heart thundering."

"I swam too hard."

"You've had time to rest. Do I excite you, Angela?"

He leaned a little closer. His lips touched the flesh of her upper arm, then crept up her shoulder and finally nestled near the nape of her neck.

"Don't you think it's about lunchtime?" she asked.

He ignored that.

"Emma will be waiting."

Still he ignored her. By now his mouth had found the hollow of her throat.

"She hates to be kept waiting."

He lifted his head and she saw the passion burning in his eyes. "So do I, Angela."

Then his mouth covered hers and she couldn't seem to control her arms. They were bound and determined to go around his neck, to caress his shoulders, to hold him close.

Then with a laugh she shook him off, got to her feet, and ran toward the water again, wading out quickly and splashing in. He came in hot pursuit, swearing softly to himself.

88

By the time they had ended their second swim, Angela knew they must go. It was too dangerous to linger any longer. She snatched up her things and walked to the car. He strode behind her, silent now. All the way to the house he was very still and seldom spoke.

Angela showered and changed into a cool sundress of green cotton, Shawn got back into his business suit, and they lunched together on the patio. Her father didn't come home. This seemed to worry Shawn, but he wouldn't talk about it.

"I'll be home early. Before five. Time for a quick flight over the island before dinner. Be ready."

She nodded. "All right."

Then he was gone and Angela both longed for the evening and dreaded it. She was losing control. It was slipping an inch at a time, but soon it was going to fly into a million pieces. She couldn't afford this. She didn't trust it. She had always been a one-man woman—had never strung more than one at a time. Now there was Michael, there was Shawn, and waiting in New York for her to phone was Phillip Blazer, her first and terrible love.

Emma had come to clear the luncheon things. Angela stopped her for a moment. "Tell me something, dear. I know you never talk about it, but I know little about the time when you were young. Why didn't you marry?"

Emma took a deep breath. "Because I couldn't make up my mind."

"To be married?"

"No, as to which man I wanted."

"Oh."

"There were two of them—brothers. I dilly-dallied between them both. They were equally charming and handsome and both liked me—but I waited too long. My little game backfired. I ended up losing them both."

"Oh, dear!"

"There comes a time when it just won't work anymore. You can flirt just so much, play the game just so long. I didn't have sense enough to know that. Anyway, if I had married one of them, I'm not sure he would ever have truly and completely trusted me. There comes a time a man wants his woman in his arms, in his house, and in his bed—without any questions of fidelity, love, or trust."

"Amen to that!" Angela said.

"And you, young lady, are playing with fire."

Angela flushed. Normally she would not have let Emma get away with such a statement. But this time she knew that the shoe fit. She was playing with fire: Somebody was going to get burned. Perhaps it would be herself!

Shawn came as he had promised shortly after four o'clock, and quickly changed out of his business suit to slacks and a polo shirt. Then, taking her camera bag for her, they went to the company car he was driving and drove to the airstrip.

"You're awfully quiet. You were found out, weren't you? They're all sore at you for going swimming," she teased.

"Something like that," he murmured. "Tell me, darling, just what angles do you want? Do you want me fly away from the sun or into it—tell me."

She told him she wanted to view the entire island first before she decided on her shots. She had seen Bella Grande from the air many times. Flying in from New York the jet always circled over the island before landing on the mainland. But she had never flown in a small plane where she could aim her camera out an open window and she was anticipating the experience keenly.

It helped to have Shawn at the controls, his hair ruffled by the breeze, his smile quick and warm. He helped her fasten her seat belt and then he revved the motor and soon the runway was skimming along beneath the wheels. He grinned again. He was in his element here. It was plain that he loved to fly.

"You should have been an airline pilot," she told him.

"I considered it," he said.

"Why didn't you?"

"Flying commercial jets is one thing, flying a little crate like this is something else. I'd hate to have to fly just one route over and over. If I want to dip down and see something, I can. If I want to land in some little airport, I can. If I want to do a loop, I can."

"Not with me aboard!"

He laughed and gave her a thumbs-up sign. "We're off."

The wheels left the ground. Her heart went with it for a moment. Then they climbed and leveled off and Shawn turned the plane toward the western sun. She saw the Gulf below, stained with silver ripples, nibbling at the white sand. The water was clear and blue with traces of green in shallow areas. She even imagined she looked down on her little cove before Shawn banked and flew over the depots of Banner Oil.

"A visual air check won't hurt either," he said.

She began taking pictures. She took all the familiar places she knew, dwelt on the beach especially, and got a bird's-eye view of Casa Linda. They were in the air more than an hour and she could have stayed much longer, but Shawn began bringing them down. She took exciting action shots of the runway coming up to meet them, of the trees growing bigger and bigger, and of the little hangar becoming more than a playhouse in the sand.

The wheels scorched the asphalt. They rolled along swiftly until they began to brake and at last Shawn brought the plane up smoothly to the hangar. He shut off the controls and grinned at her.

"Well?"

"I loved it! Can we go again?"

"Any time. We'd have stayed longer, but I have to make a phone call. Nearly forgot it. I'll use the phone inside."

Once they had climbed out of the plane, Shawn lifting his arms for her and helping her down, he strode toward the hangar. Angela paced about outside, watching the sun sinking lower in the sky. A sunset from the plane might have interesting dimensions.

She went to find a drink of water inside and she heard Shawn talking on the phone.

"Listen, Betty, it's important. You know it's important that I see you."

Angela froze in her steps. Betty! Where was he calling? New York, no doubt. And who was Betty?

"I know, dear, but we'll have to work it out some way. I have some news I must tell you. Yes, I love you, too!"

Angela had heard enough. She went outside, her imagination filling in all the empty spaces. He had acknowledged from the beginning that he liked women. He had certainly showed her that, hadn't he? She was a passing fancy, something to help while away time that on Bella Grande might have otherwise been dull.

By the time he came back, she had worked up her anger to a fine fettle. He seemed oblivious to it. He whistled as they walked back to the car and got in. He was still humming as they drove away to Casa Linda. It did nothing for her already pent-up emotions to see Michael's little car in the drive.

Shawn saw it at once and darted a glance at her. "Well, lover boy is here, I see."

"Look who's talking!" she retorted.

He gave her a puzzled frown, but she ignored it. Oh, he was good at playacting all right, good at feeding gullible women like herself a big, fat romantic line! The sultry kisses and the longing caresses and the way he'd held her! They had meant nothing. Tears stung her eyes. She shook them away. She would never let him know that he had trampled all over her heart!

Michael was waiting for her. He stood very straight, his eyes dark with anger. He gave Shawn only a fleeting glance, which seemed to amuse Shawn.

"Hello, Field. Nice evening. Are you here for dinner or just stopping by?"

"I want to speak to you, Angela," he said, ignoring Shawn.

Shawn lifted one brow and smiled to himself. He put his hand on Angela's shoulder in a very protective and personal way. "See you later," he said.

The gesture was not wasted on Michael, who flushed with fresh anger.

"Let's go around to the patio," Angela said.

"No. Away from the house. We'll walk down to the beach."

"All right. Let me put the camera inside."

"What is it? A camouflage?" he asked.

She stiffened, resenting the way he'd said it. "I was taking pictures from Shawn's plane. I think I got some interesting shots."

"I'm sure of it," Michael said. "Just how long is he going to be a house guest here?"

"I don't know," she said stiffly. "That's between Dad and him, I suppose."

"There are perfectly good rooms at the hotel, you know."

She sighed impatiently. "Michael, I have nothing to do with whom Dad invites to the house. Especially company people—"

"It's the talk of the island, not to mention the office."

"They've never talked before."

Michael stopped dead in his tracks. He gave her a hard, direct look. "Maybe there was no need for it before. It seems you've been quite often in Shawn's company. Even when I was away in Chicago."

"Playing hostess," she said with gritted teeth. "Michael, this isn't like you. I don't like it."

"Nor do I!" he said angrily.

They had stepped away from the house and Michael kept walking, looking over his shoulder now and then as if expecting to see Shawn following them.

"Do you know what you're doing, Angela?" he asked.

"I suspect you're going to tell me."

"You're making a fool out of yourself and out of all of us."

She laughed. "What a ridiculous thing to say! How can I be making a fool out of . . . just who is all of us?"

"Banner Oil," Michael said with a set, angry face. His eyes were filled with misery. She didn't understand any of this, but she felt compassion for him. Michael took everything to heart.

"I think you'd better explain that," she said.

"You know why he's here. How can you be so damned

friendly with him? What are you trying to do—save your father's neck?"

She slapped him then. Without thought, her small hand came up and collided solidly with Michael's cheek. He stared at her in surprise.

"I don't know what you're talking about, Michael, but I didn't like the implication. And for your information, I don't know what Shawn's doing here. He's from the New York office. He's making a report about general conditions. Beyond that—" She shrugged.

Michael gave her a cold, heartless laugh. "Oh, brother, Angela, you surprise me. How naive can you be? Have you got blinders on? How can you see so much in your camera, but not what's right under your nose? Shawn Stevens is here to start the reorganization."

"So—"

"It means he's going to start chopping off heads. Your next-door neighbor got it today."

"Larry Hawkins?" she asked with surprise. "He's top brass!"

"That's the beginning—only the beginning. It's rumored Harvey Davis may be next."

"Harvey probably asked for it. He shoots off his mouth all the time."

"Now you're siding with Stevens!" Michael said. "I should have known!"

"Michael, this entire conversation isn't doing a thing for me. I know you're saving your punch line. You'd better go ahead and get it over with."

"Okay," Michael said. He stopped for a moment and touched her hand. "I don't know why your father hasn't told you. Maybe the poor fool doesn't even know."

"Michael!"

"Shawn's here to take his job. Your father's on his way out."

Angela stared at him. "I don't believe it. They're friends. Shawn is our guest. They've never said a word to me about any of this."

"Ask Stevens," Michael said. "Just go and ask your handsome *caballero*. And stop making a fool of yourself with him! It won't do you or your father or me or anyone any good—"

Then Michael turned away and walked off without Angela. She stood for a long time staring out to the horizon where the sun was just beginning to settle down like an old hen covering its chicks, spreading colored feathers along the surface of the water.

So that was it! That explained many things. But why hadn't Shawn told her? Why hadn't her father?

It was time to find out a few things for herself, starting with Shawn.

Chapter VII

As she always did when she was upset or angry, Angela sought solace in the darkroom. She concentrated on developing the aerial shots from her ride in Shawn's plane. She didn't want to think about Shawn or what Michael had told her. She had always tried to keep her life separate from Banner Oil. Everyone else on the island seemed to think that their very breath could be taken only at the company's request. Granted, she hated to have her father shuffled around or let go—he had dedicated his life to the company—but at the same time she tried not to listen to gossip or petty differences that arose.

The camera was her life now. It seemed it had always been her life. The smell of developing chemicals was as natural to her as the sea breeze. Then, too, she must think about Phillip Blazer. What he held out to her was another chance, a way back to her exciting life in New York. But just how did Phillip figure into all of it? Could she trust him any more now than she could then?

The answer was to work—work hard, concentrate on something entirely different. With a little luck, all of it would become crystal clear before many more days passed.

Donning her rubber apron, closing the door, and putting on the red light, she began work. The prints began to develop in the pans and she studied them critically. Some shots were not clear. She would like to try them again. But naturally the ones she had taken of the Banner Oil Company area were very distinct. She went over them carefully, looking for details, pleased to see that her camera had not let her down.

"Funny," she murmured.

The telephoto lens had picked up some activity going on around the storage tanks that she didn't quite understand. But then she didn't know about all the operations, although she'd heard her father talk often about them over the years.

With a shrug she went on to the other prints, happy to see that Casa Linda was as attractive from the air as it was from the ground. The sea was always captivating and she could never tire of shooting it. She wished now she had had some of these aerial shots for her show. They would have added another dimension.

When she had finished her work, she went back to the house, going in through the kitchen where Emma was finishing the preparation of their evening meal.

"I was just going to call you," Emma said. "Ten minutes—"

"Okay. Has Dad come home?"

"He and Shawn are in the study, having a conference of some kind."

When she reached her room, Angela heard the phone ring. In a moment her father was calling to her down the hall.

"Angela, it's for you."

She picked up the receiver and was startled to hear Phillip's voice. "Hello, darling."

"Phillip! This is a surprise."

"Yes, I rather thought I'd hear from you today."

"I need more time, Phil, you know that. I didn't promise to phone you until I knew what I wanted to do."

"Yes, I know. But listen, I do need an answer. I've had a bit of good luck fall into my lap. I have to be in Miami tomorrow—magazine business—but I'd have time to meet with you. Will you come, Angela?"

She thought quickly and knew that nothing was going to

keep her from seeing him again. "I'm not sure I can give you an answer by then, but I'll come and see you."

"Good."

He named a time and place and she tried to quell the unbidden excitement that rose up to nettle her nerves.

Dinner was ready as Emma promised and Angela went out to find Shawn waiting for her in the hall.

"Hi," he said. "How were the pictures?"

"Most of them were good."

"I'd like to see them."

"Perhaps later."

He took her arm as he walked down the hall with her. "Your father's on the phone. He'll be along shortly."

"Just as well," she said.

He shot her a curious look. "What's wrong, darling? You seem upset. Something lover boy told you, I suppose."

"His name is Michael," she retorted.

He scowled at that. "I'm very much aware of his name and what he does and where he goes and a few other things— Never mind, tell me what's wrong."

"He tells me that you're after my father's job."

It wasn't often she had been able to surprise Shawn, but this time he came to a halt and there was a tenseness about him that told her she had hit a raw nerve.

"Michael talks too much. If I have one criticism about this whole damned island, it's that everyone talks too much!"

"It's true, isn't it?"

"I'm not at liberty to talk about company business," he said.

"Which is an easy way out for you."

"When there is anything to tell you that I am free to tell, you'll be the first to hear it. Does this mean you're angry with me?"

"Frankly, I don't know," she said.

"What has it really got to do with you and me?" he wondered. "It has nothing to do with us! I don't want to be hanged by something *they* do—Angela, you're more fair than that!"

She knew it sounded ridiculous, but how could she care about a man who was out to hurt her father? He saw the uncertainty on her face and leaned toward her. "Relax, Angela. Let's not borrow trouble."

But she couldn't let him kiss her. She moved away and she was glad to hear her father coming out of the study. The uneasy moment passed and with Emma's good food the men turned to lighter subjects—deep sea fishing, flying, and winemaking. They skipped from one subject to the other with such ease that to the casual eye anyone would think they were the best of friends.

Maybe Michael was wrong. Perhaps he was only jealous. Oh, she hoped so!

But most of the time her mind was straying to the next day when she must meet Phillip. Suddenly the idea of seeing him alone frightened her. She didn't want to make the drive there by herself. As quickly as she could after dinner she excused herself, went to get in her car, and drove to Kelly's apartment.

Kelly was surprised to see her. She took one look at Angela's face and guessed that something important was brewing.

"Better tell me before you pop a button," Kelly laughed.

She explained about Phillip's call.

"Well, it's what you've been wanting, isn't it?" Kelly asked. "You want him back. I don't think you've ever really given up."

"I used to think I wanted him back. Heavens, Kelly, I don't know anymore."

"Michael or Shawn?" Kelly wondered dryly.

She met Kelly's eyes and wondered why the truth evaded her so. When she was with Shawn, it seemed she lost all her good sense. With Michael, she felt as if she had her feet on the ground and her life under control. With Phillip—that old stirring of deep love started up again. He had reduced her to a quivering mass of humanity that didn't know up from down. Oh, the good times they'd had. She'd been at her prime with Phillip. She'd never worked or functioned better. Nor had she been so terribly, achingly alive!

"You didn't answer," Kelly prodded.

"I can't," she confessed. "I don't know. You will come with me to Miami, won't you?"

"But three's a crowd."

"I'm seeing Phillip at five for cocktails. You love to shop in Miami. We can have a binge of that before I see Phillip."

"I suppose I could look up my cousin Susan over there," she said. "Maybe visit her while you're with Phillip."

"Then you'll go!"

"Against my better judgment," Kelly said with a sigh. "But somebody has to keep you on the straight and narrow!"

No truer words had ever been spoken. As they drove away from Bella Grande the next day, Angela wondered why she had even consented to see Phillip. He had a way of making her bend to his wishes, and even with all the anger and hurt between them, when she had looked up to see him at the hall during her show, she had experienced that same old attraction.

"You know, Kelly, I'm beginning to think I'm a hopeless case," Angela sighed.

"Not you," Kelly said. "And stop talking like this. I have one thing to say and then we'll close the subject."

"Okay, shoot," Angela nodded.

"Just remember that Phillip Blazer put your heart through the meat grinder once. I'd be cautious about letting him do it again."

"I keep telling myself that," she sighed. "Over and over and over!"

Angela took a familiar route to Miami from the west coast of Florida, passing through Fort Myers and Naples and then across the state on Alligator Alley. Inland Florida was so different from Bella Grande. Here were orange groves, man-made canals, livestock, and vegetable gardens. The hot sun shimmered across the pavement, and Angela constantly looked at her watch.

"A long time until five," Kelly told her.

"Too long," Angela admitted.

Once they reached Miami, they spent their time shopping and Kelly bought some clothes. Angela couldn't seem to concentrate, even though she needed some new things.

Somehow the day passed, and Kelly dropped Angela at the hotel where she was to meet Phillip.

"I'll be back in an hour or so," Kelly said. "If you need longer, call me at Susan's."

"Okay."

Then the moment was upon her. The doorman held open the door to the fashionable hotel and Angela made her way to the lounge. Phillip was waiting outside. He got slowly to his feet and came to meet her.

"Hello, darling," he said.

He kissed her lightly on the lips and smiled at her. He was giving her that look she remembered from New York, the one designed to melt her down to her shoes. She resisted it firmly.

"You look wonderful, Angela. I wish we could have met sooner, but I just finished with my meeting and now we can have a drink. Come along, Angela. I've reserved a table."

The bar was dark, the music too loud, and the air thick with cigarette smoke. It stunned her to realize that it all bothered her. In New York she expected these things and had grown used to them.

Phillip ordered drinks and then stretched out his hand to her in a gesture that she remembered with sweet pain. She reached out to him and his fingers closed over hers.

"You're cold! Your fingers are like ice. What's wrong, darling? You can't be nervous about being with me!"

"Yes, I am," she said.

"Don't be. Pretend that we're in New York in Mac's place. Remember Mac?"

"I couldn't forget him."

"He sold cheap booze, but he treated a person like royalty the second they stepped through his door. I haven't been there lately. It's no fun without you, Angela."

She told herself that she must not pay attention to this kind of talk. It was one of his tricks to soften her up.

"And George, what about George?" she asked.

Phillip arched his brow. "George left the magazine a week after you. I thought you knew."

"Oh!"

George had been another highly thought of photographer on the magazine.

"That must have given you a few problems."

"Yes," he nodded. "But we managed. You know me, Angela. I always manage to stay afloat one way or another. But I do miss you. More than I ever thought I'd miss anyone."

"So you want me back."

She was bemused by this thought. She used to lay awake at night dreaming how he would come to take her back. Not that she had ever expected it to happen, and he certainly wasn't begging now, but at least he wanted her.

"Yes," Phillip sighed. "I want you back. You're good on the magazine, but more than that, I want you back for me, Angela."

"Oh, if only I could believe you!" she murmured.

"What did you say?"

She lifted her head and gave him a bright smile. "I said, that's very nice."

Their drinks arrived. She drank hers far too fast. She felt a little dizzy.

"Bella Grande is a pleasant diversion—for a little while," Phillip said smoothly. "But I can't believe you want to spend the rest of your life there. Listen, baby, the whole world is out there waiting for you. You have new avenues to travel, new frontiers to reach, and you're going to get better all the time. I liked what I saw in your show, darling, and I meant what I said about it."

She let him talk. She leaned back and tried to relax and just listen. Phillip was too smooth and too smart to dig a hole he couldn't get himself out of. So what he was saying had to be taken at face value. She began to believe what he was saying and the longer he talked, the more she wanted to reach that feeling of greatness. What would it be like to be world renowned? To be sought after, to be highly paid, to be . . .

She laughed.

"What is it?" Phillip asked. "What's so funny?"

"You spin a very attractive web, Phillip. But that's what it is, a web. How does the victim ever escape the spider's web?"

"If you don't aim your camera at something, you won't be happy," he said bluntly. "It's a part of you, Angela. Sometimes I think you have film for muscle and developing fluid for blood. And you're not going to find what you want anywhere but New York. I'm the one that will take you back there and open doors."

"Will you give me more freedom on the magazine?"

He flushed. "All I can. But there is the publisher to contend with, you know. He has final say—and if you go too far afield . . ."

"There's not that much new and fresh you can do with a model and a designer gown!" she retorted. "But at least you could let me strike out for something better."

"If it's better, we'll like it," Phillip nodded.

Then suddenly he stopped talking about the magazine. He turned their conversation to the personal side. He told her he had missed her more than he thought he'd miss anyone. He longed to phone, but his stubborn pride hadn't let him. He had written countless letters, only to throw them aside.

"I don't know what I would have done if Janice hadn't told me about your show and given me a valid excuse to come."

"I wish I could believe that, but I don't," she said coolly.

He swore. He ordered another drink and drank it quickly. Then he ordered still another and drank that. He smoked nervously, lighting one cigarette from another.

"What more do you want from me, Angela? A proposal of marriage?"

She stared at him when he said that. Phillip had made it plain from the beginning that marriage was not a part of his plans. Love affairs, yes. Cozy relationships, yes. But a wedding ring—no never!

"You'd hate being married," she said.

He lifted his shoulders in a shrug. "Maybe I'm getting old, Angela. Maybe I'm changing my way of thinking. The least you could do is give me a chance."

"Maybe," she said.

"Then you'll come?"

"I didn't say that. I won't tell you today. I never make a decision that fast."

"You did when you left me and came back here," he retorted.

"Self-preservation. You were destroying me, Phillip."

"You were always so damned serious about everything. You should know that games are played, games that mean nothing."

"I hate that," she said. "Maybe I'm square. Maybe I'm not in tune with you and your New York ways—but I hate that!"

"Don't say no. I didn't arrange this meeting to hear you say no."

"I won't say no, but I won't say yes either."

"The thing of it is, we need to be together, Angela. To grope our way back. To give us some time, some way to level off."

She didn't want to talk about it anymore. Her head was spinning. Her heart was being pulled two ways at once.

"I have a room here in the hotel," Phillip said. "Maybe we should go up there—away from this racket. We could talk easier."

"No."

"Such modesty!" he teased.

"I don't want to be alone in a hotel room with you, Phillip. I don't trust you."

"You know me so well," he said. "I would like to hold you in my arms, Angela. Maybe if we could be close . . ."

She shook her head. She didn't want to be in his arms.

The moment she did that— She gripped her glass with icy fingers. She had to keep control, to step carefully.

Phillip looked at his watch. "Time goes so fast when I'm with you. I hate to tell you, but I have another appointment in a few minutes."

"Kelly will be coming by for me anyway. It's been nice, Phillip."

"Nice," he said tightly. "Yes, nice!"

He walked with her out to the lobby, put his arms around her for a moment, and kissed her. The room tipped and she was glad that someone was calling to him.

It was a woman, a very impatient woman.

"Be right there," Phillip called back to her.

Angela gave him a cool smile. "Your appointment is not pleased because you're keeping her waiting."

"Phone me, Angela. Promise me—soon."

"Soon," she nodded.

Then she turned away, not wanting to see Phillip go to the other woman and take her arm and turn on that charm of his. She doubted that the woman was a business appointment. But it could have been. That was the worst part of being with Phillip. She was never certain of him, never able to completely trust him, not after Deloris—that other woman—who had made havoc out of their lives.

Kelly appeared five minutes later and Angela was glad to get into the car and head west toward Bella Grande once again. They drove through the city traffic and out again to Alligator Alley before Kelly asked her how it had gone.

"I don't know. The more we talked, the more confused I became. Maybe he's sincere. He even talked about marriage, but I think that was just a ploy."

"Different for Phillip."

"Too different," Angela decided. "I'll have to give it some real thought."

"I expected you to fold up at the sight of him and simply let him talk you into anything."

"You should know me better, old friend," Angela said. "Once I get a case of the stubborns, I don't buckle under very easily to anything."

They had a bite of supper together on the way and talked about girlhood days and other problems they had faced.

"Usually we've been able to hash them out between us," Kelly said. "I hope you decide to stay the summer on Bella Grande. We can have fun like we used to."

"I thought you were taking some summer courses at the college."

"I am, but they won't take but a few days a week. There will be plenty of free time."

When they reached Bella Grande, they parted with plans to get together soon. Then Angela drove home to Casa Linda. Only a single light burned in the living room, so she knew that Emma was probably alone.

"Emma!"

"In here, dear."

Emma was watering her precious geraniums.

"You haven't had a bite to eat!" she guessed.

"But I have."

"We had dinner late tonight. Your father came home to eat and then went right back to the office."

"Oh, I see. And Shawn—has he gone back to New York?"

"No. He didn't come home with your father. Seems there are some problems."

"I'll bet!" Angela sighed.

She went to her room and changed into slacks and sandals, but she felt restless and tired from her meeting with Phillip. When the doorbell rang, she was almost glad to see Michael, even though they had parted in anger at their last meeting.

"I have to talk to you, Angela."

"Come in."

He looked past her into the house. "Are you alone?"

"For the moment."

"I think I'd rather go for a drive. Okay?"

"Why not?"

They went out to Michael's little car and drove away from the house. He talked about several things, none of them important, but he seemed on edge and finally brought the car to a halt at one of the lanes off the main road, where they could point the car toward the Gulf.

"Emma said you went to Miami today. I called earlier."

"Yes, Kelly and I."

"Shopping?" he wondered idly.

"Shopping," she nodded.

"Nothing more?"

"Why are you questioning me?" she asked angrily. "All right, I met Phillip! Satisfied?"

Michael tapped the steering wheel with impatient fingers. Then with a sigh he leaned his head back and closed his eyes. He looked tired. There were dark circles under his eyes, and despite herself and her anger with him, she felt a touch of sympathy for him.

"I'm sorry. I didn't mean to answer like that. But I do have to resolve a few things with him, Michael. My old job has been offered—they can't wait forever—I have to make up my mind."

"I see."

"I'm at loose ends here, Michael. Even though I've been busy, even though I could work freelance with Bella Grande as my home base, I need something to keep busy. I was never one to idle away my time."

"Yes, I know," he said. He gave her a slow smile. "Look, honey, I owe you an apology. I came down hard on you the other evening. I know I threw you a curve, too. I should leave Banner gossip at the office."

"I think that might be wise."

"I just thought Stevens was stringing you along and you didn't know what you were getting into, that's all." He touched her hand. "Understand?" he asked anxiously.

"Sure," she nodded. "It's all right, Michael."

He stretched his arm along the seat behind her and touched her shoulder with his fingertips.

"The trouble is, we've not been together, not really together, in what seems like years."

"Years," she murmured.

He pulled her close and she dropped her head to his shoulder. It felt comfortable there and as he wrapped an arm snugly around her, she felt safe. Perhaps the way to go was with Michael. He would love and cherish her forevermore.

"Stevens was responsible for giving me a little more time here. But you knew that, didn't you?"

"Yes, he told me."

"How did that come about?" he wondered. "It isn't like Stevens to do anybody any favors."

"Would you mind not talking about it anymore? Frankly, I'm sick to death of the Banner Oil Company!"

Michael laughed. "I don't blame you. Sometimes I am too. So, tell me, what would you like to talk about?"

"Anything!"

He tightened his arm around her and dropped a kiss to the top of her head. "All right. I have something to discuss. I've been giving it a lot of thought, darling. You know how I feel about you."

"Scared to death sometimes," she teased.

He laughed. "True. Because I'm always afraid you're going to come and tell me you're leaving the island."

"That could happen any minute," she said frankly.

He turned her to him, and in the fading light of the day he met her eyes. "You can't go without me, darling."

"But you'll probably spend the rest of your life right here."

He shook his head. "No. I have a line on a new job, Angela. With another oil company, but the same line of work I do here. I think I have a good chance of getting it. It's based in Chicago. They approached me when I was there a few days ago."

"You're not serious!" she said with surprise. "I thought you were a true blue Banner idiot!"

"I used to be. But I don't like what I see happening. It would give us a fresh start and, darling, I want that. Could you be happy in Chicago?"

She thought of that windy city with its stubby skyscrapers and choppy lake and shook her head. "I don't think so."

"Don't put it down. There's a lot of opportunity there. More than you might expect."

"Maybe, but not for me. It's either New York or California, if I go anywhere."

Michael kissed her lips for a long moment, stopping her words. "But as my wife, you might be happy. I'd do everything to make you happy, darling, you know that."

She lifted her head to look fully into his eyes.

"Dear Michael!"

"What's that mean?" he wondered.

"I'd make your life miserable."

"I'd risk it," he said with a smile. "I'd be a fool not to. A woman like you comes along in a man's life only once. I know that. I want you, Angela. More than you can ever know."

She reached up and kissed him, but there was no real excitement for her, no soaring of spirits. Nothing like when Phillip had kissed her and lately—Shawn.

"Don't give me an answer yet," Michael said. "Because I can see no written all over you. Think about it. And remember how much I love you."

He started the car then and they drove on aimlessly, enjoying the night, watching the stars in the darkness. She thought about José. There were times she was tempted to take Michael there. Somehow she knew José would approve of him, but she held back. That particular part of her life on the island was very private.

They turned at last toward Casa Linda, having driven to the far end of the island. The music on the radio was relaxing. Angela felt sad and couldn't imagine why.

As they neared the house, Angela saw bright lights piercing the black sky. At first she thought it was from the airfield, and then she realized it was coming from near the oil depot.

"Michael, what is that?" she asked.

He had seen it too, and watched for a moment. He tightened his lips.

"I don't know. But maybe we'd better find out!"

"Dad should be home by now," she said. "Let's stop there."

Michael wanted to go straight out to the depot, but gave

in. He began to drive faster and they reached Casa Linda in a few minutes.

Rushing inside, they found Edward Wales just hanging up the hall phone.

"Trouble at the depot," he said with a worried frown.

"We saw the lights," Michael said. "What is it?"

"One of the tanks is leaking oil. We have to stop it. Drive me out there, Michael."

"Sure."

"I'm going, too!" Angela said.

She took time to dash to her room for her camera and her flash unit. They were waiting impatiently for her as she climbed into Michael's car. Her father had crammed himself into the tiny back seat and was plainly on edge.

"Those tanks are old. I've been worried something like this might happen."

"Why hasn't the head office done something about it?" Michael asked.

"I don't know. It's not because I haven't reported it—I have. Shawn has too. But it's very possible they've sat around on their hands a little too long. Can't this little crate go any faster?"

Michael shoved down the gas pedal and the car leaped forward. They raced toward the depot. There were cars ahead of them and cars behind them.

With Angela's father in the car they cleared security in a matter of seconds. Then they drove as close to the scene as they could.

"Damn!" her father muttered.

Then, cramming a hard hat down on his graying head, he took off on a run. In a moment Michael had shed his coat, tossed it into the car, and followed him.

Security guards were keeping the curious onlookers back and they held Angela back too.

"Can't let you pass, Miss Wales."

"What happened? Do you have any idea?"

"No. Haven't heard."

She crept away from the guards and tried to find a way through the line, but it didn't work. They kept chasing her back. She had to content herself with photos taken from some distance away, but she used her tripod and honed in on her subject with her telephoto lens. It was impossible to tell what she would get. She had never filmed anything under such conditions. But stuff like this made good photographers.

Sometime during her camera work, she spied Shawn in the midst of the workmen, a hard hat covering his black hair, his shirt covered with oil and grease.

He was shouting something, in full command, and she began clicking the camera, knowing that she was catching Shawn's fierce personality on film. He was a lion all right, caged and angry. She saw the fury written into every line. But she saw something else, too. She saw fear.

Chapter VIII

The confusion grew worse. There were shouts, urgent instructions, desperate voices, and men and equipment came pouring into the area. Michael had disappeared, not to be seen again, and from the sidelines Angela couldn't tell exactly how serious the matter was. Only Shawn's face had driven shafts of fear into her heart.

Then suddenly Shawn was beside her. His face was grimy with oil and there was a small cut just above one eye. He gripped her hand tightly, leaving an oily smudge.

"Take your father home, Angela."

"What's happened?"

"It's no place for him. We have plenty of men here now. I'll appreciate it if you'll just get him out of here."

"But why?" she demanded angrily. "He has every right to be here—the same as you—more than you!"

He was quickly angry and impatient with her. "Take him home. He's worn himself out and I need him by the phone. The New York office has been notified and they'll be wanting to get back to us. Impossible to do that from here—tell him to handle the calls and if necessary, relay them to me here. Got it?"

Then Shawn was gone and the security people let her through long enough to locate her father. He was in the thick of things and annoyed to find her so near the dangerous oil leak.

"Get back, Angela. My God, I thought we had better security than this!"

"Shawn wants you to go back to Casa Linda. Man the phone there—they're expecting calls from New York."

He stared at her, swallowing hard. She could see the indecision in his eyes. He wanted to stay more than anything, but with a sigh, he nodded.

"Okay. We'll go. We can use Shawn's car."

"Where's Michael?"

"God knows. Haven't seen him. But he's in the thick of things, I'm sure."

"Has the leak been contained?"

"We're working on it," he said. "The big danger is fire, Angela. One spark—one tiny little spark and . . ."

His voice went as hollow as his eyes. She took his arm and tugged him away. Once inside Shawn's company car, they drove away quickly from the turmoil and Edward Wales leaned back with a tired sigh.

"I'm not up to these crises anymore, Angela. I must be getting old."

"That's a lot of poppycock if I ever heard it," she retorted. "But you could use some clean clothes and a cup of coffee. Let the men do the hard work; you use your head—manage things from the house."

"I suppose you're right," he nodded. "Sometimes I wonder why I ever got into the administration end of the business."

She supposed it was no time to mention it, but she couldn't hold back the angry words.

"I wonder why Shawn Stevens seems to be the man in charge instead of you," she said.

Her father sighed and rubbed at his oily hands with a soiled handkerchief, thumbing back his hard hat. The hair that peeked out was gray and seemed to be turning whiter every day.

"I suppose I have to tell you sometime. It's possible, even probable, that Shawn will be taking over here."

Her pulse jumped. "And you?"

"Undecided. Maybe they'll just let me out to pasture, Angela."

"A good man like you? Wait until I give Shawn Stevens an earful! If he's so stupid as to let you go—"

Her father patted her hand to silence her. "Let's not belabor the point now. Let's not air it around, either. Even though everybody is second-guessing Shawn's intentions, let's keep cool."

"I wish I had been blessed with some of your level-headedness," she confessed. "Okay. We'll keep cool."

Emma nearly fainted when she got a good look at her employer. Angela laid out some clean clothes while her father scrubbed up in the bathroom. By the time he'd changed, the phone was ringing. For half the night the phone rang constantly, and Angela found herself acting as courier. Something had happened to the phones near the tanks. Even the security-guard house was without communications.

She handed Shawn the first message personally and he read it anxiously.

"Great lot of good that will do!" he grumbled.

"What's wrong?"

"New York's sending down a team of experts to tell us what's happened—hell, we already know what's happened."

"Enlighten me."

Shawn sighed tiredly. "The tank simply sprang a small rupture. There's a lot of pressure—I don't know how we've been lucky enough to keep it from springing more leaks."

"I want to know why the phones aren't working. Am I to be kept trotting back and forth like some racehorse?"

"Some filly," Shawn said, his eyes raking her up and down.

"Well—what is wrong with the phones?"

He took a deep breath. "Someone cut the wires—precaution, I think. In case it would generate some kind of spark—there's always that little touch of electricity, you know—God knows, even the tiniest spark . . ."

Then he was gone, answering someone's shout and Angela wanted to stay and watch, but she knew that at Casa Linda her father might be needing her again.

114

It was a long, long night. At about four in the morning the phone stopped ringing. Things were under control at the depot. A crew was left behind for safety's sake to keep their eye on things, and Shawn came home shortly afterward.

Emma had been sent off to bed, but Angela had kept a pot of coffee going. Shawn looked as grimy as all the workmen when he came into the house. She saw that his knuckles were bruised and bleeding and that the cut on his forehead had opened up more.

"Better tend to that," she said.

"I'll shower first. Man, that coffee smells good."

"How do you like your eggs?"

"Sunny-side up. And I think I could eat a whole pound of bacon, too."

"Okay."

Her father, assured by Shawn that things were under control, had finally said good night and gone off tiredly to bed.

Shawn wasn't in his room long. When he came back, he looked scrubbed and shiny, a maroon satin robe over his fresh-smelling body.

"Would you mind?" he asked. He held out his bruised hand.

"I'll get the first-aid kit," she said.

At the kitchen table, with the eggs and bacon waiting, she tended to his small cuts and bruises. He winced under the antiseptic and fought the idea of a bandage on his forehead.

"Not that important."

"You get an infection in it and then you'll think it is very important," she said. She opened up the small bandage and slapped it on. "Matter of fact, it makes you look dashing."

He smiled tiredly at that. "I'll just bet it does."

She dished up the food and he ate it hungrily. She began to think that he would never stop eating.

"Almost as good a cook as Emma," he said. "That's nice."

"You're just hungry enough to eat anything," she retorted. "Is there any more danger now?"

He looked at her point-blank for a long moment. "You saw through me."

"Yes. I think Dad did, too, but he was so tired, he was ready to accept whatever you wanted to tell him."

"We've made temporary repairs to the tank. Maybe they'll hold, maybe they won't. If they don't, I expect the whole damned thing to go. Do you have any idea how much oil that will be spilling out around the tanks, out into the sea? Your beautiful white beaches may be ruined. We'll lose marine life, the beach, boats, and homes. Not to mention the loss of the precious oil."

"Can't it be pumped out?"

"Every tank is full. We're trying to get a tanker to come—no luck yet."

"Why was it allowed to happen?"

"I don't know," he said. "I really thought those old tanks were going to last a while longer. They were getting near the danger point, but I didn't really think . . ."

He broke off with a sigh and held out his coffee cup. "A little more, please. Then I'm going to try and get some sleep. An hour or so. Would you awaken me then?"

"Shawn—"

"I'll never hear the alarm," he said. "I'm just about out on my feet."

He managed the coffee and then with a grin that completely disarmed her, he got to his feet and motioned to her to walk with him. He put his arms around her shoulder.

"Just the right size. You ever notice how you fit there?"

He never made it to his bedroom. As they walked through the living room, he collapsed onto the sofa.

"Oh, man—" he murmured.

She fluffed a pillow and tugged him around so that he was more comfortable, but even then his feet hung over the edge. There was simply too much man for the couch. He whispered something sleepily to her, grasping her hand in his.

"What did you say?"

"Don't go away," he murmured. "Stay close—"

Then his eyes were closed, his breathing was deep and even, and he was out. But when she tried to loosen her fingers from his, he hung tightly, not wanting to let her go.

"Shawn—"

"Love you—" he whispered.

"What? What did you say?"

His eyes came open for a split second. "You heard me."

Then he really was asleep. She finally sat down on the floor and leaned her head against the couch. All the while he slept, he clutched her hand. Only once did he relax enough for her to wiggle free. She ought to go to bed, she thought. It had been a long night. But it was oddly comforting to be so close to this big, nice-smelling man who had sacked out in his robe, his hair still damp from the shower.

She must have fallen asleep too. When she awakened, she had a crick in her neck and the phone was ringing.

She yawned loudly and stumbled to answer it.

"Hello."

"Shawn Stevens, please."

"One moment."

She went to shake him awake. It took a couple of hard nudges before he finally stirred.

"Telephone. I think it's one of the men."

He was instantly awake. He went to take the call and Angela looked at the clock on the wall. Seven. Emma was in the kitchen and she smelled coffee. Shawn's voice on the phone had suddenly become very reserved. He was standing so still and she sensed that he didn't like what he was hearing. When he hung up, he gave her a brief glance and went to get dressed.

"Want to check it out, even though they said it's okay," he said. "Then I'd like to relax for a while. I've been hearing about a certain stretch of beach called Sereno—they say it's particularly lovely."

"Yes."

"Meet me there about ten. For a swim."

"I'm not sure."

"Meet me there," he said. It was an order now. "I have to talk with you."

Then he rushed away, peeling off his robe as he went. She caught a glimpse of big, broad shoulders, suntanned and powerful, before he disappeared down the hall.

Her father was getting up. By the time Emma had breakfast ready, he was dressed for the day, looking tired but prepared.

All through the meal Angela was conscious of a tension in the air. Yet the two men seemed on friendly terms, talking about the oil leak and the way the Banner people had leaped in to help.

"You have a good bunch here, Edward," Shawn said.

"Yes, I have. Glad you could see that last night."

"And Angela, your Michael did himself proud."

Angela's brows went up. "My Michael?"

He gave her a long, searching look. "Isn't he?"

Her father cleared his voice and quickly changed the subject.

After they'd gone off hurriedly to the oil depot a few minutes later, Angela tried to phone Michael, but he didn't answer. Knowing him as she did, she wouldn't be surprise if he were still at the accident site giving his all.

About nine thirty, Angela put on her swimsuit and drove to Sereno Beach. She really didn't think Shawn would come. There would be too many details to handle—New York people to meet, questions to ask, reports to be made out. But she was there and she would enjoy the beach whether he came or not. It was probably the most ideal place on Bella Grande for swimming in the Gulf.

It was one of those clear, lovely days and the water was as clean and pure as ever. How they had contained the oil leak, she didn't know. She was just glad that they had.

For a while she stretched out on her beach towel on the sand and let the sun drift over her, touching, caressing, and easing away the tightened muscles of fatigue. She dozed once, awakened, saw that Shawn had not come, and dozed again.

By now it was well past ten o'clock. She was both angry

and glad that he hadn't come. She needed this time alone, she supposed, to think about Phillip. Why was it she couldn't even conjure up the contours of his face right now? All she could see were palm trees swaying in the breeze, the surf rippling and foaming white across the sand. She watched the sea gulls and decided she might as well go out and enjoy the water. It was too tempting not to.

She waded out, the water feeling cool against her hot, sunbaked skin. Soon, she began to swim leisurely, pacing herself so that she could go a long way if she chose. She was enjoying the water, relaxing, when suddenly an arm came out of nowhere and caught around her.

She screamed, thinking for an ugly, horrible moment that a shark had attacked her. Then she saw Shawn's wet head and his wicked grin.

"Got you!"

"Why didn't you call out? You just took ten years off me."

He laughed at that, his teeth flashing white.

"Want to go farther or go back?"

"Back," she replied. "And I don't want to race you either. I want to enjoy every moment of this."

"Okay."

He paced himself to her strokes and they swam in unison.

"Hey, we look pretty good," she called.

"Perfect," he said.

When their feet touched sand at last, they waded out, shaking off the sea water, and headed for the towels left on the beach. Shawn stretched out tiredly beside her, his face to the sun.

"How can you come here like this?" she asked.

"I have until two o'clock. Then the company plane will land with a bunch of New York people and all hell will break loose."

"Too bad."

"You certainly sound sympathetic!" he retorted with a grin.

"I couldn't care less," she said. "To be very frank—"

119

"Sorry. I shouldn't talk about the company. Not when I have you all to myself. We have this beach, the sun, the wind, and if you're thirsty—there's a bottle in the car."

"No thanks."

"Don't need any stimulus?" he teased.

Looking at him, his long lean legs, his narrow hips, his broad shoulders—he was the epitome of the well-built male figure and she was having a hard time keeping from staring.

"You're dissecting me, my love," he grinned.

"You should pose for a centerfold in one of those women's magazines," she quipped back.

He shrugged. "Would you buy one of them if I did?"

"No."

"Ah, I know—you would do the photo yourself."

She went red to her toes and he laughed. Then he got up and walked to his car parked under a palm tree nearby. He came back with an ice bucket that she recognized as belonging in Emma's kitchen.

"She loaned it to me," he explained as he sat down beside her on the beach. "It didn't take much persuasion. Emma likes me."

He uncorked a bottle of something bubbly. "It's not champagne. I have to keep a clear head. Only ginger ale. But I thought we could pretend."

He poured two glasses and they sipped it, eyeing each other over the rims. Shawn's eyes watched her with growing adoration.

"I wish I didn't have to meet with those officials this afternoon. I would like to spend the entire day here with you."

"You would be burned to a crisp if you tried that."

"I'd risk it. Later we could move under the palm trees. We could find a place, sheltered, where there would be no one to see us."

"Oh?"

"I'd want no one to see us. What I have in mind, my darling, is not for curious eyes."

She heard the passion rippling along his words and his hand came out to caress the smooth skin of her arm. His fingers felt cool, and as they moved up to her shoulder, nestling under her hair, she felt an answering tingle. Slowly he put his glass aside, took hers from her hand, and set it away too. Then he leaned over her and his shoulders covered her. His face was there, his mouth coming down on hers. The kiss was long and ardent, and she found that as usual she couldn't resist him. With a groan she gave him back his kiss and then he was nuzzling her throat and moving down to press his lips to the crevice above the line of her swimsuit.

"Don't," she said. "Don't, Shawn—"

"Yes," he murmured. "Yes."

She felt a need, a longing, and in another moment she came abruptly to her senses. With a laugh, she gently pushed him away.

"I think we'd better take another swim—to cool you off."

"Just me?" he asked with a quizzical lift of his brows.

She was off and running, tucking her dark hair under a bathing cap. Soon he was pounding beside her and he took her hand as they waded out into the surf. With a laugh, they plunged in and she felt the salt water, cooler than her skin, and put her face into it, concentrating on swimming. They didn't go far. Shawn stopped her after a few quick strokes. There in the water he put his arms around her. They went underwater and there he held her close. She was glad when they came up for air.

She went back toward the shore and he came with her. Once there, she picked up her towel and dried off. He retrieved his glass and drained the clear liquid.

"You're not going!" he said with surprise.

"Yes."

"But we have another hour—more."

"I think I'd better get back to the house."

His eyes were flashing with a mixture of anger and despair. "Stay, Angela. Please. We'll walk on the beach. I won't touch you again."

"I know better than that."

He gave her a twisted grin. "You're probably right. What are we going to do about this, Angela?"

"Nothing."

"It will burn us both out. It will be murderous to be near each other and not . . ."

"I suggest you move out of the house and go to the hotel."

He got slowly to his feet. "You're not serious."

"Oh, but I am."

"What do I tell your father?"

"Whatever you like," she replied quickly.

He began to fold his towel as well, lazily stalling, keeping her there. "The truth?"

"I've found it's usually best, but this time, I think not. I'm not sure he'd like to know that you're—you're—"

"That I'm attracted to his lovely daughter, that I find I'm eager to have her in my arms every chance I get? That I daydream about her when I should be working? That I have trouble at night knowing that there are only a couple of walls between us? That I could open her door and find her there in the night—perhaps waiting for me?"

"Shawn, don't say these things!"

"If you're such a lover of the truth, you might as well hear," he said. "I want you, Angela Wales, and one way or another, I'm going to have you."

She lifted her chin. "Against my will?"

"I'm not at all sure it would be against your will. Can you deny it, Angela? You want me, too."

She walked away then, afraid to trust her voice, unable to find anything wry or witty to say. It seemed best to get into her car and drive away. But he was coming behind her and before she reached her car, he was striding beside her, his arm around her shoulder.

"It will soon be lunchtime. Come and have lunch with me at the club."

"Emma is expecting me."

"We have to stop by the house to change anyway. We'll tell her. Emma's a good scout. She won't care."

"I think it's best I not see you again, Shawn."

"You don't mean that."

"Don't push me, Shawn!"

"Only moments ago you were lying in my arms and

happy to be there. In another moment you would have—"

"I would have done nothing!" she said with clenched teeth. "Why do men always leap to the conclusion that women are just dying to fall into their arms and be made love to?"

He grinned at that. They had reached her car and he tossed her things inside. Then he reached out and twisted a finger around a lock of her dark hair.

"Because it is usually true."

"Male chauvinist!"

He looked steadily at her. Then he backed her against the side of her car, and with one motion he lifted her as he had more than once so that they were eye level.

"Keep it up, Angela, and I'm going to have to teach you a lesson."

"Let me down, Shawn."

He shook her playfully, like she was a little kitten to be teased.

"Kiss me good-bye first."

"No."

"You're afraid."

"Never," she shook her head. "But I really would like to go now and you're not being very nice."

He grinned wickedly. "I never claimed to be."

"From the beginning, Shawn Stevens, you've been some kind of a devil, do you know that?"

"And from the beginning, the minute I saw you at the airstrip, I knew you'd be a handful. But what a sweet handful."

He leaned toward her, but she turned her head. He swore.

"Angela, don't try my patience."

"You're hurting me, you know. You grip me so tightly, my ribs are bruised!"

But he didn't let her down. Finally, to be rid of him, she allowed him to kiss her. Despite all her defenses, all her determination, she found herself weakening again. In a moment, her hands had reached out to caress the back of his neck, to tangle in his thick hair. Then he picked her up in his arms and moved away from the cars.

In the shelter of the cool palm trees, he laid her down. His eyes were burning with desire.

"Darling, darling."

"No, Shawn."

"Try saying yes for once. Don't spoil this beautiful moment with resistance. Surrender to me, my love, now."

It would have been easy. Far too easy. But she knew that this must end. She must not see him again, be alone with him, for inevitably it would come back to a moment like this.

"Don't do this, Shawn."

"You might as well talk to the wind."

"I don't like being just another woman."

His eyes began to glow dangerously now. "I never said you were."

"From the beginning you admitted that you liked women, that you were the kind of man that chased anything in a skirt—"

His lips quirked upward. "Not just anything—give me more credit than that!"

Her cheeks were burning. "Then there is Betty . . ."

He was stunned. "Betty!"

"It's no use, Shawn. This is over—now—this very minute."

"What do you know about Betty?" he asked incredulously.

"Oh, I heard you on the phone, talking so sweetly, saying you loved her. What kind of fool do you take me for, Shawn Stevens?"

She walked away then and he didn't try to stop her. But he was furious.

He had knotted his fists and he stood tensely watching her as she climbed into the car, spun the wheel around, and roared down the lane away from him, not once looking back.

Angela's heart was thudding hard and her nerves were fine pieces of steel wire, stretched to the breaking point. Her head began to throb and she clenched the wheel so tightly that her nails poked little breaks in the skin of her palms.

At last Casa Linda. It looked more welcome than she had ever known it to look. But soon Shawn would be coming behind her and he would be there under the same roof, a temptation, a man who could melt her down to nothing with just one touch of his hand.

I can't lose control like this, she told herself. *I can't be near him—*

She tried to think of Phillip, of New York, her work. She fastened her thoughts desperately on Michael, but none of it worked. It was only Shawn that filled every nook and cranny of her mind and her heart.

She reached the house and went quickly inside to her room to shower off the salt water and get dressed. She thought she heard Shawn's voice, but she wasn't sure. The thing to do was stay in her room until he had gone to the office.

But she wasn't that lucky. A shadow appeared at her glass door and Shawn stood on her patio. The door wasn't locked, but it wouldn't have done any good anyway. Shawn was going to see her whether she wanted to see him or not.

He had changed into his business suit. He stood very tall and masculine, a furrow cut across his forehead, and as he stepped into her room, she stood her ground.

"I've come to tell you of my decision," he said.

His words were coldly controlled, but his eyes were hot and burning.

"Yes," she said coolly, trying to treat him as a stranger.

"I've asked Emma to pack my things. I'd do it myself, but there isn't time. I'm due at the office in a few minutes. The New York people are arriving sooner than expected."

"I see."

"I'll move into the hotel. I'll tell your father some kind of story—I don't know what yet."

"I'm glad," she said.

"You'll miss me."

"No."

"Hell, Angela, don't try my patience any more than you already have!"

"Don't expect me to say things I don't mean."

She stared at him coldly and he returned the look. In a moment he had strode across the room to her. His hands gripped her shoulders tightly and he peered into her eyes.

"You're some kind of tease, is that it?"

"And you—what are you, Shawn? I'm just a diversion to pass long, boring hours."

He let his hands fall and stepped back from her. She worked hard to keep her face haughty and indifferent. He swore to himself then, moved to the door, and yanked it open.

"They say there's a fool born every minute," he said. "I guess that's true."

She gave him a curt nod. "Oh, yes, I believe that."

She was the fool for letting it go this far. His eyes were sparking with fury now and he closed the door with a hard push that echoed through her room. He stalked away and a few minutes later she heard him leave the house. His car spun its wheels as he drove off.

Angela pressed her forehead to the cool glass of the patio door, where only seconds ago he had stood. She had sent him away thinking badly of her. Just as well. She didn't want him near, couldn't bear the thought of him in the house, couldn't trust herself to resist him again. No, it was better that it end like this. Let him go back to Betty or some other woman.

Shawn Stevens did not belong in her life. But who did? Phillip? Michael?

"I don't know," she admitted.

But she knew that she had to decide soon. She had to get her life together.

Chapter IX

Angela ate very little lunch that day, and Emma gave her a long, thoughtful look but didn't say anything. She knew something was wrong and she didn't quite understand Shawn's sudden decision to leave the house, but Angela couldn't tell her anything now, couldn't bring herself to talk about it.

She left the house herself shortly after lunch, her camera slung over her shoulder, and she began walking toward José's house. Thomasita was on the beach, building a fort complete with cannon and came running to meet her, nestling her brown hand into Angela's.

"Hi, Angela! Want to see what I'm making?"

Angela spent several minutes admiring the structure and making a suggestion or two. Then, with Thomasita skipping beside her, they went up to the cottage. José was mending the porch, his hammer and saw noisily mixing with the sound of the surf and the squawk of the sea gulls.

He gave her a friendly grin and put his tools aside to sit down beside her on the step. He filled his pipe and she watched his work-hardened hands as they tamped the tobacco into the bowl.

"Been scarce around here lately," he said with a grin. "Maybe it's because of that new fella—Shawn Stevens."

She flushed and José laughed, knowing that he had hit the nail straight on the head.

"I've also been to Miami to meet Phillip. I can have my old job back, José."

He lifted his brows at that and blew a smoke ring. Thomasita rushed to push her finger through it before it was swept away on the sea breeze.

"Are you going back to New York?" José asked.

"I don't know. You're looking at the most undecided girl on the island."

"Maybe you been here too long, got your brains sun-baked," he grinned.

"I've done something all right. I suppose you know all about the big excitement last night."

"They were lucky," José said. "Could have been a lot worse. Wonder what happened."

"Old things break. Those tanks have seen better days."

"Maybe," José nodded.

She gave him a quick look. José always knew everything that was going on around the island. She sensed now that he knew more than he was telling.

"What is it?"

"Just talk, *poca minina*."

"Are you going to pass it on?" she asked, nudging his ribs playfully. "Stop teasing!"

He shrugged. "Okay. There's *mucho* talk—maybe it wasn't just an accident."

A chill rushed over Angela's body like a splash of cold ocean water on bare skin. "Sabotage?"

"Maybe. But I suppose the bigwigs will decide that, won't they?"

"But why? Who? I don't understand why anyone—"

"Plenty of mad fellas in the company now. Don't like what they see coming. Maybe somebody is a sorehead."

It was a new idea, a startling thought. She wondered if Shawn was aware of this. And Dad? Funny, she had been living in the house with two top Banner executives and José picked up more on the street than she knew!

"Did you ever just want to get away from it all, José?" she asked with despair.

He nodded at that. "Sure. Many times. I get in the boat and go. You want to go fishing?"

Thomasita jumped up and down at the idea, but Angela shook her head. "No, but I have a better idea. Maybe I'll go visit Aunt Franny in Tennessee."

"Maybe you should," José said. "Sometimes, it's good to put distance between fire and tinder."

"Am I the fire?" she wondered, always startled at how well he read her and her problems.

"You're the tinder," he said quietly.

They talked for a while longer before Angela said good-bye. Thomasita walked with her as far as the gates of the courtyard of Casa Linda.

"Are you going away?" she asked.

"Maybe for a little while. But I'll be back. I'll bring you a present."

"Promise?" Thomasita asked with a big smile.

"I cross my heart," Angela said.

Angela gave Thomasita a quick hug before the little girl ran back down the beach toward her grandfather's house.

Now that the idea had begun to take root, Angela took quick action. A long distance call to her aunt in Tennessee brought the welcome she expected. She checked with her father to see if there was a company plane going in that general vicinity. She had caught rides like this before.

"I'll check, darling," he said. "I'll let you know tonight. And I think it's great you're going to see your aunt."

"Dad, how are things going there?"

"I'll talk to you later, dear."

He hadn't answered her question. Either he was evading it or he was unable to talk. Someone might have been in his office at the time.

Angela loved her aunt Franny, but she lived a very quiet and secluded life, even though the Gatlinburg area was designed for tourist trade. Still, Franny kept to herself in the little mountain house on the hillside and Angela decided it would be fun to take Kelly with her.

With this in mind, she drove to Kelly's apartment and discovered her painting her kitchen a bright, sunny yellow.

"Hi," Kelly said. "Grab a brush."

"No, thanks. When are you going to finish this?"

"In a couple of hours. How do you like it?"

"Nice. Kelly, I have an idea. I thought you might like to go with me to visit Aunt Franny."

Kelly looked at her with surprise. "I thought you'd given up the idea."

"I have it again. I want to go. Tomorrow."

"Tomorrow! Gee, I don't know, Angela. How long will you be away?"

"A week, ten days, maybe two weeks. We'll play it by ear. You could skip those summer courses a couple of days, couldn't you?"

"They haven't started yet. I do have a couple of weeks before they begin. Let me think about it."

"We could have a lot of fun, Kelly. Promise you'll go."

Kelly climbed down off the stepladder and laughed. "I'll see. No promises. Besides, I've got a feeling you're going off on some kind of camera binge."

"I haven't filmed the mountains in quite a while," she admitted. "I probably will take a few shots—"

"A few!" Kelly scoffed. "With you, it's always a million. You get to be a lousy bore about it all."

Angela grinned at her friend's frankness. "I'll try to control it. Honest."

But Kelly still wouldn't promise and Angela left her to finish her painting. Now that it had been decided she would go, she began to feel more and more enthusiastic. Fresh horizons, new people, different sights. It had to work. It had to put her head back on straight.

She spent the rest of the day searching through her closet and tossing things into her flight bag. Then she developed some tag ends of film and looked at the prints. Once again, she reviewed the aerial shots of Bella Grande taken from Shawn's plane, studying those of the oil depot with more and more interest. Those men around the tanks—somehow she had always thought there was something odd about them. Could they have been the saboteurs? But they wouldn't have been doing anything in broad daylight! She tossed the photographs aside once again, picked up some film from her dwindling supply, and locked up the room.

By the time her father came home in the evening she

was restless and eager to be on her way. He gave her a quick kiss and put his arms around her for a moment in a rare display of affection.

"What's that all about?" she asked with a laugh.

"It's been a long day. It's cleared for you to go to Gatlinburg tomorrow morning. Eight o'clock. I'll take you to the airstrip. A company plane will drop you off. It's on its way to Chicago anyway—no trouble."

"Good! Dad, about the trouble down at the depot—"

His face tightened and she saw a weariness come to his shoulders. "They're trying to blame me. As general manager, I am responsible for all conditions."

"Baloney!" she said heatedly. "You've been after them for months to replace those tanks."

"It seems they overlook that part of it. Let's not talk about it now. I'm starving. Does Emma have dinner ready?"

He was changing the subject on purpose, but he looked so tired these days that she didn't press. Still, she longed to ask if what José had heard was true.

They had barely finished dinner when the doorbell rang and Emma went to answer it. In a moment Angela heard Michael's voice.

"Come in, Michael," her father called.

He stepped into the room, wearing slacks and a casual sport shirt. Angela forgot sometimes how attractive he was in his own way.

"I'd like to take a walk, Angela, or go for a ride. I want to talk to you."

Her father excused himself and went to the study where he closed the door. Angela had watched his tired steps and felt an overwhelming compassion for him.

"Michael, what's happening?" she asked.

He had guessed her concern for her father and shook his head. "A lot of things. But I didn't come here to talk about Banner Oil."

She sat down beside him and he put his arms around her shoulder and kissed her forehead. "Darling, have you thought about what I asked you the other night?"

She stirred uneasily and realized that she hadn't even

given his proposal of marriage a second thought. How could that have been? It wasn't every day a woman was offered a wedding ring.

"I'm going to Tennessee tomorrow, Michael."

He stiffened with surprise. "Are you running away from me?"

"Myself," she admitted. "I need some time to think."

"And when you come back?"

"I'll tell you," she said. "It's only fair."

He looked at her with hope in his eyes. "I wish you weren't going. I wish—"

She shook her head. "No, it's all planned, Michael."

"And knowing you, there's no point in trying to change your mind."

She reached out to take his hand. "That's right. Let's walk out to the pool. The breeze will be cool now. We can watch the sun go down."

They walked through the house to the patio and sat down in comfortable lawn chairs beside the aquamarine pool.

"This is a lovely place," he said. "I hope someday I can own a home like this."

"You've never told me about this other job—"

He shook his head. "Nothing definite."

"You'll never leave Banner Oil," she teased.

His eyes flashed angrily. "Don't be too sure. If Stevens is going to run the show . . ."

"I thought you agreed that he was fairer than you'd expected."

"Maybe. Then why am I suspect, why is every decent, hardworking employee at the Banner Oil Company suddenly being watched, questioned, and made to feel like some kind of criminal?"

Angela saw the despair on Michael's face. "The oil leak—"

Michael set his jaw. "Yes. It's supposed to be top secret that they suspect sabotage, but everyone knows about it. And Stevens seems to think that I especially should be watched."

"I don't believe that!"

132

Michael's eyes were reaching the danger level now. "He's given you a snow job, my pretty! He's out for no good. Your next-door neighbor has a for sale sign in his yard. Did you notice? He's leaving the end of the week—shipped off to some little ratty job in the Midwest—all due to Stevens and his broom. He doesn't care who gets hurt, including your father."

Angela's nerves tightened. "What about Dad?"

"Nothing definite, but there's more talk every day. And now with this trouble, they've really gotten some leverage to use against him. You know company politics. It's a dirty dog-eat-dog business, and Stevens is as bad as anyone else!"

She got to her feet and moved away to the pool. "I don't want to talk about it."

"You're in love with him, aren't you?"

She was stunned by this question. She had never told Shawn she loved him. Had never let herself even think of this possibility. There was a physical attraction she couldn't deny. It came burning between them whenever they met. But was it love?

"I don't want to talk about Shawn," she said. "Please, Michael. I'm going away tomorrow. Can't we part on a civil basis?"

He relaxed then and took a deep breath. "I'm trying, Angela. More than you know."

She felt sorry for him. He seemed so on edge these days and she knew she wasn't helping the matter. He came striding toward her and touched her hand.

"Want to go to the yacht club?"

"And hear more talk about Banner Oil? No, thanks!"

"How about golf?"

"No."

"Tennis? We can use the schoolyard courts—avoid the crowds at the club."

"That might be fun."

"You're on!" he said with a pleased grin. "I have some tennis shoes in the car, the racquets, too."

"I'll change. Only be a minute."

He waited for her around the pool while she went back

to her room and put on her tennis shorts and shoes. She tied her hair back with a bright ribbon and was ready.

Angela always enjoyed the intensity of tennis. She liked to meet the demands it made on her wit, stamina, and concentration. It was an excellent way to tone her body and brain and ease her tension at the same time.

Michael whistled as they drove away from Casa Linda, and she found his good nature contagious. She began to feel lighter of heart, and when they reached the courts, they found Kelly and her friend Pete Ryan there.

"Hey! How about a game of doubles," Kelly called.

Michael got the racquets out of the car and nodded. "You're on, pipsqueak."

He always teased Kelly like this and she responded with a healthy retort that made everyone laugh.

Pete Ryan was a quiet young man, likeable enough but Angela didn't think he was right for her friend. Kelly needed someone with more life, more vim and vigor. Still, he batted a mean tennis ball and he and Kelly consistently showed her and Michael how the game was supposed to be played.

"Pretty hot stuff, aren't you, Kelly?" Michael asked.

Kelly made a face at him. "The trouble with you, Michael, is that you have two left feet."

"Want to take me on—in a singles game?"

Kelly shrugged. "Why not? Want to put a little money on the side?"

"If I win, you treat me and the rest of us to champagne."

"And if I lose?"

"I treat," Michael said.

They began a fast and furious game and Michael kept pace with Kelly. Kelly set her face in determination and they called each other terrible names across the net. Sometimes Angela wondered if Kelly meant some of them, but Michael set his jaw, clutched his racquet all the tighter and put his concentration to work, letting her abuse bounce off him.

"This may go on forever," Pete told Angela, looking at

his watch. "I have to be back at the office in twenty minutes."

"This time of day?"

"Yes. Afraid so."

"Can't you stay and see how it will end?" Angela asked.

"Not this time," he said. "Listen, will you and Michael see Kelly home?"

"Sure."

Pete called to Kelly that he was leaving and she held up her serve long enough to bid him good-bye. Pete put his arms around her and kissed her for a long moment. Michael stood impatiently, getting angrier by the second.

"Come on, break it up! Are you playing tennis, Kelly, or smooching?"

Michael's taunt made Kelly angry. She detained Pete longer, kissing him still another time. Michael swore. His face was getting red and his temper was flaring. Angela was a little surprised by this. Michael was not one to care much about what other people did.

Finally Kelly let Pete go, blowing him a kiss as he went.

"How sweet!" Michael murmured.

"Shut up," Kelly retorted.

Once Pete's car had disappeared around the school-house, Michael gave Kelly a very hostile look. "You're really not going to fall for him, are you?"

"What's it to you?"

"He's not right for you. And he's not going to last at Banner Oil. He's not sharp enough."

"I think he's very nice!"

"He's a deadhead!"

Kelly was furious. She charged toward the net and Michael met her there. They argued heatedly for several minutes until Angela went to break it up.

"What's with you two? Now come on! Michael, Kelly's personal life is her business. And you shouldn't talk about poor Pete that way."

"Poor Pete!" Michael said incredulously. "You don't know anything about him, Angela."

"And neither do you!" Kelly retorted. "If it's all right with you, we'll call this game off, right now."

"We have a bet on!"

"Forget it," Kelly said.

Kelly began gathering up her things and all the while Michael kept challenging her. Kelly turned back with one parting shot. "Go soak your head, Michael Field!"

Michael was so stunned by this that for a moment he couldn't come up with a reply. By now, Kelly was walking off the courts.

"Wait a minute," Angela said. "We're going to take you home."

"I'll walk," Kelly told her.

"Come on now! We have to talk about Tennessee. You're coming with me, aren't you?"

Kelly paused and gave her a quick look, watching Michael out of the corner of her eye. "Hey, I meant to call. I was going to later. I've decided against it."

"But, Kelly—"

"Have fun," Kelly said, gripping Angela's arm for a minute in a friendly clasp. "I'll see you when you get back."

Then she hurried away, avoiding Michael as he came dog-trotting toward them. He watched Kelly go and shook his head.

"I guess she really got sore, didn't she?"

"You weren't very nice. What's with you two? Every time you're together, you end up fighting!"

Michael shrugged. "I guess we rub each other the wrong way. Did I hear her say she wouldn't go with you tomorrow?"

"That's right. And I want you to look her up and apologize," Angela said. "Promise."

He shrugged. "Sure. I guess I did come down a little heavy. It's just that she's a sweet kid—I'd hate to see her louse up her life with a guy like Pete."

Michael persuaded Angela to play a couple of games before they went home. She worked off a lot of restlessness by swatting the ball with all her strength and chasing around the tennis courts. Michael played to win.

"Enough," she said at last. "And it's time to go. I have some packing yet to do."

136

"Okay."

They went back to his little car and, as they drove to Casa Linda, he took a detour by Kelly's apartment. A light was burning and he grunted his approval.

"She made it home okay," he said.

"You really do like her, don't you, Michael."

"Sure, she's okay," he said in an offhanded way.

At the door of Casa Linda, Angela said good night.

"I'd like to come in," Michael said.

"No time. I'll see you when I get back."

"Phone me from Tennessee?"

"Sure. And don't worry about things, Michael. It will all work out."

"With Stevens at the helm?" he said bitterly. "You're kidding yourself."

"Shawn Stevens is not a vindictive person!"

"And you're the expert, I suppose," Michael said quickly and angrily. "Maybe some of the gossip about you two is true after all."

"Michael, don't do this," she said wearily.

"I'm sick and tired of hearing you stand up for that man!"

"And I'm tired of hearing you constantly run him down!"

They glared at each other. With that Michael turned on his heel and stalked away. Angela took a deep, weary breath. What was happening anyway? Why should she defend Shawn when all the odds were against him.

Michael had gone off in a huff. It seemed they were fighting all the time these days and she was not the sort who usually did that. She couldn't think about it now. Tomorrow—she would think only of tomorrow.

Casa Linda stirred early the next day. Emma knew of Angela's plans to leave and had promised her a good breakfast.

"As if Aunt Franny has no food in the house," she had teased.

Emma smiled her knowing smile and went right ahead with her own plans. But Angela was surprised to find they had guests for breakfast, their next-door neighbors, the Hawkinses. They were leaving the island the next day and it was apparent from their long faces that they were not happy about it. Edward Wales tried to make the breakfast a festive one, but it fell flat. Angela watched him struggle to keep the conversation going and knew that he felt bad about their transfer.

"We've been here together a long time, Edward," Larry said. "Now—everything's changing."

Angela lifted her chin. "José says it's the nature of things—to change."

Larry gave her a grim smile. "I suppose so. I know that our lives will never be the same. Bella Grande is our life and now . . ."

She knew they blamed Shawn. She wondered if they ever considered the fact that he took orders from higher up. No, they didn't! She listened to the gossip and the talk and the rumors until she thought she would scream.

She was saved by the mere fact that if she didn't say good-bye and leave, she was going to miss the company plane.

"I'll drive out myself, Dad," she said. "Someone can pick up my car later."

"No, I'll take you," he insisted.

"Stay with your guests," she replied. "I'll phone you tonight. Good-bye everyone—"

There was a round of handshakes and a kiss or two and then with her father's help she stowed her belongings into her car and drove away.

The sun was brilliant, the ocean clean and pure. She wondered if Thomasita was already hard at work building sand castles and if José had finished the porch. Laughing to herself, she knew that she was homesick for the island before she had even left it.

The ten-minute drive to the airstrip took her less than eight. She pushed the car hard down the asphalt road, and when she saw the hangar ahead, she pulled under the shade of a tree. Snatching up her belongings, she carried them to the building and looked around. There was no company plane here!

"Well, hello."

She turned around to find Shawn. Their glances were cool and didn't linger.

"If you're looking for the company plane, there's been a change in plans."

She lifted her chin. "How's that? Dad said it was all arranged!"

Shawn strode toward her. He was wearing a light summer suit and a bright tie, and his black hair was glossy in the sunlight. She had not seen him since he had packed his things and left the house, but everything was very familiar, even the little line at the corner of his mouth as he smiled, the sound of his footsteps, and the devilish light shining in his eyes.

"The plane isn't going," he said.

"I knew I should have taken a commercial flight! Maybe I can still get one——"

She picked up her things and started away, but Shawn stopped her with a hand on her arm.

"Not so fast. You didn't let me finish. Why do you always fly off the handle and never listen?" he demanded.

She felt nettled, as if she had just fallen into a batch of sandburs.

"What is it you have to say, Mr. Stevens."

He cocked a dark brow at her. "*Mister* Stevens!" he said with a low, roguish laugh. "So, it's like that, is it?"

"I want to know about the plane! I don't have time to stand around here forever!"

"Running off to Tennessee," he said, gloating.

"I have an aunt there. I haven't seen her in ages and the Smoky Mountains are lovely this time of year. Green and cool——"

"Oh, sure!"

She flushed. He was putting this all on a personal basis and she hated every minute of it. She looked at her car just a few steps away. Right now it seemed several miles. But she must get away from him quickly. She was far too conscious of him standing there, tall and handsome, his big shoulders blocking out the view of the airstrip.

"I have to wait for a phone call," he said. "Then we'll be on our way."

"We?" she asked as scathingly as she could.

"I'm flying you. I'm off to Chicago on business. We'll go in my plane."

"I think not."

"Don't be an idiot," he said coldly. "I can have you in Tennessee before you could ever find a seven-twenty-seven to board on the mainland. Calm down. You'll enjoy the ride, I promise you."

"Just who's idea was this?"

"It just happened, honey."

"Did Dad know—"

"Probably not," he said with a shrug. "But it doesn't matter, does it, as long as you get to go."

"Are there any other passengers?"

He grinned and swept his gaze over her. "No one but you, dear. Just the two of us. It will be real cozy."

"Sometimes, Shawn Stevens, I think I hate you!"

He tilted his head slightly, but her angry words hadn't made the slightest dent. He didn't believe her. Thinking about past times with him, she felt hot and uneasy. She had never acted as if she hated him—at least not for very long.

He took her things and stowed them in his plane. Then he spent a few minutes in the cockpit, checking controls and gauges. Angela paced about restlessly, wondering how she had gotten herself into such a mess.

"Chicago," she said. "Business, you said?"

"Right," he nodded.

"What about the oil depots? Did you catch the saboteurs?"

His gaze narrowed. "What do you know about that?"

"Rumors are everywhere. Did you really think you could keep something like that a secret on Bella Grande? If so, it's because you're green, unseasoned. You don't know island life."

His face colored and she knew she had hit a raw nerve.

"Dad should have handled it," she said airily. "There would have been far less trouble and talk that way."

He set his jaw. "Do you have anything else to say?"

"Only that if this plane doesn't leave in five minutes, you can forget about me as a passenger."

Just then they both heard the phone ringing in the hangar. Shawn gave her a triumphant look.

"It seems you lose, Miss Wales."

He walked off to answer it. He was taking a very long time. Angela paced about, stared at the sky, looked at her watch, and tapped an impatient foot.

Finally she went to see if she couldn't hurry him along. He was still on the phone, his back turned to her, and he was laughing.

"Of course, dear. I think it's an excellent idea."

She heard the mellow tone of his voice. She had never heard him sound so benevolent and sweet.

"I'll be in touch with you soon about it, darling," he was saying.

Another pause and he murmured something she couldn't hear. Angela remembered another phone conversation she'd overheard, one that had haunted her ever since. She knew instinctively that it was the same woman on the line.

"I love you, too, Betty," Shawn was saying.

He was about to hang up. Angela moved away quickly and in a moment or two he came striding out of the room. He paused for a second when he saw her.

"I'm ready now," he said. "Come along, Angela."

He tried to take her arm, but she shook him off.

"I'm not your darling Betty," she retorted.

He stared at her for a moment with surprise. "I always forget that you like to eavesdrop." Then he began to smile. It twinkled out of his eyes and broke out into a laugh on his full lips. It was very, very funny to him. But beneath, down deep where she let no one see, she was crying and hurting and wishing that she had never laid eyes on the likes of Shawn Stevens.

Chapter X

Behind her Angela could hear Shawn's stride, his quick, impatient steps, and in a moment or two they had reached the plane. He helped her up and into the passenger seat. There was room for two more people, but that was all.

"Fasten your seat belt," he said.

"I already have."

"Good. If the lady is ready to fly, so am I."

She turned her head to look down at the airstrip and wished he'd get them airborne. She had a feeling it was going to be a long way to Tennessee!

Shawn taxied the small plane out to the runway and soon he was revving up the engine and the wheels were flying down the asphalt. Just when she was certain they would end in the drink, the wheels lifted off and they soared into the air.

"I like this moment the best," Shawn said. "I love that sensation of leaving the earth behind."

She was in no mood to make small talk with him, but on the other hand, she didn't want him to realize how upset she was over Betty either. She became absorbed by the sight of Bella Grande falling away beneath her, a tiny place in the huge ocean. Was that the tiled roof of Casa Linda? Could she possibly pick out José's modest little cottage?

"It looks so vulnerable down there all by itself," she said.

Shawn nodded. "Getting a bird's-eye view of places gives them different perspectives. When I'm flying I realize how small I am, how terribly insignificant."

She darted him a look. "But you love to fly!"

"Yes. Maybe it's because I realize that I'm truly a part of the universe, even if I am a mere speck. God's in his heaven and all's right with the world."

She was a little surprised by this line of conversation, but soon it turned to more mundane topics.

"There's a nice place to eat in Atlanta," he was saying. "We might stop over long enough for an early lunch."

"I understood this was a direct flight," she replied quickly.

He lifted his shoulders in a lazy shrug. "Okay, but we'll be stopping there for fuel. There's a Thermos of coffee. I didn't have time for breakfast. Would you mind pouring me a cup?"

The Thermos was full and there was a brown bag filled with sweet rolls from the hotel's coffee shop. She poured the coffee and, at his insistence, joined him.

"We have a perfect day, Angela. Ever see the skies so clear and blue?"

"Beautiful," she nodded.

"Look," Shawn said with a scowl. "You might as well sit back and enjoy. Surely this small plane doesn't make you nervous."

"Frankly, I'd prefer the seven-twenty-seven."

"But this is cozier."

She shot him a look filled with fire. "I'm not interested in being cozy. I'm interested in getting there in one piece."

"Never smashed a plane yet," he said with a grin. "I don't plan to this trip. I'll be checking the weather ahead as we go. If there are thunderstorms, we'll go out around them. Enjoy the flight, little angel."

"I'm not a little angel! Not by a long way."

He laughed at that and she wished that they weren't so confined in the small plane. He could reach out and touch her without trying and there was no way to escape him.

He did so that very second, his hand cupping her knee in an all too familiar way. With cold fingers she took his hand away and he laughed.

"Devil!" she said in a smothered voice.

"Never claimed to be anything else," he said.

"Please, just concentrate on your flying!"

"No problem," he told her. "I know this old bird inside and out and I know what she'll do under almost any circumstance."

She concentrated on the coffee, hot and delicious. Perhaps the altitude was effecting her appetite. She devoured one of the sweet rolls, too, and Shawn lifted his coffee cup to her.

"That's more like it. We have several hours together, honey. I'd hate to think we were going to fuss all the way to Tennessee."

"Are you sure the weather ahead is okay? I heard on the radio that Atlanta was going to have rain, that it was coming from the northwest."

"I'll check," he said, "just to put your mind at ease."

He spent the next several minutes on the radio and got weather reports that sounded good all the way to Atlanta. "No rain there. You're going to be all right, honey."

He was teasing her now, gently poking fun at her. Normally she loved flying. Maybe it was just that she felt uneasy being with Shawn. She would be glad when they would arrive in Gatlinburg and he would fly on to Chicago.

She wondered idly what he was going to do there and asked him.

"Business," he said. "Company business."

"Something about the sabotage?"

"Indirectly. And I wish you'd stop calling it that. We're still not certain."

"Okay. Maybe you'd rather tell me about Betty."

He gave her a long, devilish look, his hazel eyes sparkling with mischief. He nodded.

"I'd be glad to. What do you want to know?"

"I suppose she's beautiful."

"To me, she's the most beautiful," he nodded. "She has

144

charm, character, good looks, personality—you name it, she's got it."

"Blond?"

"Matter of fact, she is."

"Well stacked?"

He cocked his head. "Never thought about it before, but yes, she is."

"Never thought about it!" she scoffed. "You always size up a woman from head to toe. I know your type."

"You're trying hard to make the day pleasant, aren't you?" he asked sarcastically.

"I don't like being strung along."

He stared at her. "Nor do I! Every time I turn around, there you are hanging all over Michael Field."

"We're old friends."

"So you've told me," he said wryly. "Friends? Just friends?"

"I resent the implication."

"Dammit, Angela, I don't like having to ask."

She lifted her chin. "Then don't!"

He turned his attention to flying. She sat stiffly beside him, watching the patterns of the land beneath them, picking out the houses snuggled in the country, the cluster of buildings that made up small towns, and the antlike movement of autos and trucks on the strips of white that were the highways. Flying at a lower altitude than she was accustomed to on the large jets, she could see much more and felt closer to Mother Earth. They passed over an orange grove—acres and acres of trees laid out in a careful pattern.

Then Shawn pointed to the right. "Disney World. Want to stop?"

"No, thanks."

"We could be kids again for a day."

"But when the day was over—"

He looked grim for a moment. "Yes, we'd be adults again and all the problems would still be there."

They soared on and he pointed out the cities as they went.

"How do you know all of this?" she asked.

"Pilots have maps, like auto drivers have roadmaps."

"Tell me when we leave Florida."

"Will do," he nodded.

He was on the radio several times, but there was still no reports of rain ahead. The skies were becoming hazier, but he told her it was a typical summer condition.

"What will you do in Gatlinburg?" he asked.

"Kelly accused me of planning a camera binge. I probably will photograph everything. I usually do when I visit a different place, not that I haven't already filmed most of the highlights."

"Do you have friends there?"

"A few. Not many. Mostly Aunt Franny."

"Is she like your father?"

"No, very different," she replied.

"Do I get to meet her?"

Shawn gave her a quizzical look and she knew that he was testing her. "No."

He pretended to be wounded, holding his hand over his heart, looking full of anguish. "How can you do this to me? It's only common courtesy."

"I realize that taking me to Gatlinburg is slightly out of your way. I know that I must be a bother."

"You're determined to pick a fight, aren't you? All I wanted to do was meet your aunt!"

"I'm quite sure that my family—none of them—is of any real interest to you."

He set his jaw. "You're referring now to your father, aren't you?"

"I just know, Shawn Stevens, that ever since you put a foot on Bella Grande, everything's gone haywire!"

"Heap it on!" he sighed. "My shoulders are wide."

But he wasn't going to talk about his work with Banner Oil or what the long-range plans were. He deftly turned the conversation and began telling her how he had first learned to fly.

"I had a friend who had served in Vietnam. He was a pilot and operated a small place where he gave flying lessons. I took to it like a duck to water. In fact I turned down a chance for a job with him."

"Maybe you should have taken it," she quipped.

He sent her a look that tingled along her nerves, despite her determination to resist him. "But then I might never have met you. Think what a loss that would have been."

"Lord, you're full of it, aren't you?" she retorted.

"You never found it offensive before. Why have you suddenly turned on me?"

"I haven't turned on you. I just don't like some of the things you do."

"But you like some that I have done," he told her slyly. "I remember lying in the sand with you in my arms. I remember how you held me, how you kissed me—I rather think you enjoyed it, Angela."

"I don't want to talk about it."

His hand was on hers, covering it warmly. "Going to have to one of these days," he said.

"If you can tear yourself away from Betty!"

He laughed at that and kept laughing until she was fuming. She had no idea what was so damned funny about it all.

The radio sputtered and he answered the call. The conversation did nothing to lift her morale. Rain was beginning to fall in Atlanta, a fine mist. The weather on to Tennessee was not going to be good.

"We could wait it out in Atlanta," Shawn suggested. "This summer weather usually clears in a few hours."

"If at all possible, I want to push on," she replied. "Aren't you due in Chicago?"

"It could wait a day if necessary. We'll decide when we put down at Atlanta."

She was fuming at the thought of a possible delay. If only she'd used her head and simply refused to fly with Shawn in the first place! A large jet wouldn't have let such a smidgin of weather stop them. A small plane was another matter.

The mist started a short time after they'd crossed the Florida border and stayed with them all the way to Atlanta. They had to circle the airport for another few minutes before they were cleared to land.

"It will probably take an hour to fuel up and get ready

to continue, if we're able to continue," Shawn said. "We'll find something to eat."

They went into the terminal together and found their way to a coffee shop. In a booth they looked at menus and Shawn ordered a large meal. To her dismay she heard him ordering the same thing for her.

"I can never eat all of that!"

"Sure you can. We have plenty of time to enjoy it."

Shawn was wearing a green knit shirt, slacks, and a sport jacket. His hair was brushed and glossy and more than one admiring woman glanced his way. But he seemed to ignore them and focus on her.

Leaning away, he lit a cigarette and smiled. "Would you like one?" he asked, holding out the pack. "No, thanks," she snapped. They're not Belair longs."

He frowned. "We're not operating on the same wave-length today, are we?"

"No."

"Because of Betty?"

She lifted her chin. "I don't like being one in a stable of women. Sorry, I don't play that kind of game."

He grinned. She hated it when his eyes flashed, and his message came tumbling across her heart like leaves in a high wind. He took her hand and raised it to his lips, kissing each finger, at last putting a final kiss on the palm of her hand.

"You're special, Angela. You're not like any other woman I know."

"I wonder what's keeping the waitress. Where's our food?"

He dropped her hand with an air of disgust. "I thought you weren't hungry."

"I think I'll go to the powder room."

She left him in the booth, smoking impatiently, angrily. In the ladies' lounge she took her time, fiddling with her hair, applying fresh lipstick, looking at her watch. She wished she were in Gatlinburg right then. When she knew she couldn't delay any longer, she went back to the table.

Their food was waiting and growing cold. Shawn rose to

his feet and his shoulder brushed her arm as she slid back into the booth. He sat down beside her.

They ate silently. He didn't seem to have his usual appetite and she wasn't hungry at all, but she forced herself to eat.

As he paid the check later, Shawn picked up a few candy bars and thrust them into his pockets. He'd also ordered some sandwiches and had his Thermos refilled.

He left her in the waiting room and went to check on the plane. Angela couldn't sit still. She paced about, watching the people as they scurried to make their planes or walked into the room with someone to be greeted or to say good-bye. Airports were fascinating places, slices of life. She felt the itch to get her camera, but she had left it in the plane.

"It's ready."

Shawn had appeared silently beside her. As they walked through the busy terminal, he took her arm. His touch burned her skin, but she wouldn't let him know.

"It's still raining," he told her, "not heavily and they think we'll soon run out of it as we bend a little east to Gatlinburg. Unless you're afraid to push on . . ."

"No!"

Due to the weather, heavy traffic, and delays in takeoff, they sat on the runway more than half an hour before they were cleared from the tower.

The little plane seemed to hum unevenly, but Angela was no expert and was certain she was imagining things. Soon they had cleared the runway, their wheels off the ground, and they banked and turned once again toward the green hills of Tennessee.

Shawn was busy at the controls, talking with the tower as she watched out the window. The day was gray and dismal now. Rain obliterated most of her view. The cabin began to feel close and oppressive.

"How much longer will we be?" she asked.

"Another hour and we should be close. Depends on this rain. I thought we might circle around it, but it seems there's not much chance. The weather system is moving faster than they had first expected."

"I wish we were down on the Gatlinburg runway," she said uneasily.

He gave her a quick look. "Listen, honey, everything's okay. This weather isn't bad at all. I've flown in fog thicker than pea soup and through winds of almost cyclone velocity. Relax!"

She didn't want to admit how nervous she was becoming. How foolish she had been not to insist they stay in Atlanta until the weather had cleared. Better to have spent a long and dull day in the terminal than to be aloft, beginning to shiver with an unexplained fright. She had never believed in premonitions, but she couldn't shake this feeling that something was going to go wrong.

Shawn had grown quiet now, handling the plane with his usual efficiency, but a tiny little frown had appeared above his eyes. Now and then he seemed to be glancing at one of the gauges.

"What's wrong?" she asked anxiously.

"Nothing. Nothing to worry about."

"There is something wrong!"

"Gauges do malfunction, you know. In fact this one has acted like this once before. Nothing to be alarmed about, honey."

"You're lying to me!"

He shot her an angry look. "Listen, I don't have the time to argue with you about foolish things. I have a plane to fly and weather to contend with. I don't need anything more!"

"I'll shut up!" she shot back.

He took a deep breath and she was braced for his retort when they both heard the engine start to sputter and then stop. Shawn moved into quick action, trying desperately to start it again.

"Damn!" he muttered.

"Shawn—"

"This is a twin engine plane," he said evenly. "We'll make it in okay. Nothing to worry about. It will slow us down and you'll have to put up with my charms a little bit longer, that's all."

"You're lying to me. Please, Shawn, don't do that. I want to know what's going on."

A burst of lightning slashed the air just then. An air current caught them and sent them into a sudden dip that made Angela clutch for something solid.

"Air pocket. Nothing's wrong, sweetheart. We're okay," Shawn said, bringing the plane level again.

But she didn't believe him. They were in a storm that was steadily growing worse, approaching the mountains of Tennessee with only one engine. Even before she could complete the thought, there was another bolt of lightning, closer this time, and Shawn had stiffened with tension beside her.

"Going to try and get away from some of this, darling," he said. "Hang on."

He began to bank, but it was as if the storm was chasing them, surrounding them, determined to choke them off from blue skies and smooth flying.

"The storm's getting worse," she said.

He got busy on the radio, trying to pick up a small local tower somewhere, but there was no answer.

"Out of range," he said. "With this electrical storm— but we'll reach someone soon."

"Are we lost?"

"No!" he said emphatically. "Just off course a little. But we'll get back on it in a few minutes."

"Shawn, I don't like this. I'm scared."

He reached out and put his arm around her for a moment and pulled her close. "Don't be. I'll take care of you, sweetheart. I won't let anything happen."

But the storm had other ideas. The rain was coming in torrents now. They were flying blindly, relying entirely on instruments and they were not staying on a level course at all. The wind was fierce. It battered them around like a Ping-Pong ball during a hurricane.

Then, as if they hadn't enough to contend with, the lightning seemed determined to track them down. It cracked and snapped so near that she was certain they'd been hit.

"Shawn—"

"I'm going down," he said with a hard jaw. "Maybe we can find a place to set down until this blows over. Here, keep calling for help. Tell them it's a May Day."

"May Day!" she said with alarm. "Shawn—"

"Hate to tell you, honey, but we're losing power. I think that last bolt of lightning got some of my electrical system. Get on the radio, sweetheart, while I try to handle this baby."

The plane was sinking fast now. She could feel it falling like a leaf through the sky. With shaking hands she handled the mike, shouting for help, yelling, "May Day, May Day, May Day!"

The plane was vibrating and Shawn's face had gone stony quiet, tense with concentration.

They were falling, falling, falling! With supreme effort, he somehow brought them out of the dive and she saw the trees of Tennessee, black and dense with rain beneath them.

"Look for a place to put down," Shawn yelled at her. "A highway, an open field—anything—we only have a few more minutes . . ."

But there was nothing! Nothing at all! Just solid trees, a mass of dense forest.

"Get those pillows," Shawn said in a tense voice. "Put them in front of your face, you know the position for crashing—do it now, Angela!"

"But you—what about you—"

"Shut up, Angela, and for once in your life do as someone tells you. Save that pretty face of yours—"

She found the pillows in the seat behind her, stuffed them between her and the cockpit, and prepared herself for a rough landing.

Shawn was shouting at her now. "I love you, Angela. I love you—"

Then the trees were there, directly in front of them, ripping at the wings, tearing at the wheels, crashing against them with the most terrifying, horrible sounds she'd ever heard.

They were smashed and torn and bounced around

through the trees and then there was one final crash and she heard nothing more.

She had no idea how long she had sat doubled over in the cockpit, but then she felt someone shaking her gently.

"Angela, are you all right? Angela . . ."

She lifted her head slowly. She seemed to ache all over. There was something sticky on her forehead and she reached up to find blood streaming down her face. She was dizzy and her eyes wouldn't focus, but she could see Shawn bending over her. There was a terrible bruise on his face, and one eye was swollen, but he was alive. She began to cry and he put his arms around her, patting her.

"We're down, honey. In bad shape. The plane's a total wreck. We have to get out of here. Can't stay inside. Always danger of an explosion, gas tanks are probably ruptured. Come on, darling."

She didn't remember how they got out of the plane, only that Shawn was there with strong arms lifting her and helping her as she tried to walk deeper into the shelter of the trees away from the plane. The rain was steady, the wind no longer gusting. The worst of the storm was passing by now, but it had thrown the bird to the ground and broken its wings.

Shawn led her under one of the pine trees, helped her sit down, and put her back against the trunk. His eyes were compassionate, hollowed out with pain.

"So sorry, darling. Stay here. I'll be back in a few minutes. I'm going to try and salvage some things from the plane—we're going to need them."

She closed her eyes clutching her hands into the good soil of the earth, and thanking God she was still alive. She felt her arms and legs. Nothing broken, only bruised ribs, a cut on the forehead, this crazy wooziness.

Shawn was gone for a long time. Perhaps she slipped off into unconsciousness again, she didn't know. When she opened her eyes once more, she saw him coming. Her focus was better now. She saw he had his arms full of blankets and pillows and the Thermos was tucked under his arm. Coffee—she'd sell her soul for a cup of hot coffee just about now!

Then she realized that Shawn was limping very badly, that every step was torture from him. She got unsteadily to her feet.

"Shawn, you're hurt—"

"Ankle—my knee—"

He was a few steps from her when he collapsed. With a cry, she went to him unsteadily, nearly falling, struggling on. By half dragging him, persuading and begging him to help her all he could, they got to the tree where big branches offered them refuge. With shaking hands she spread a blanket, making him lie down on it and covering him with another. By now she could see that his foot was badly swollen. He cried out with pain whenever he moved his knee.

"Big help," he said thickly. "God, Angela, I don't know how I could have gotten us into such a mess."

"We'll stay here until the rain stops. Rest, Shawn. Try to rest."

"I gave a May-Day call on the radio several times, but I'm sure it wasn't working—thought I'd give it a try anyway."

"Will anyone have heard us? Do you know where we are?"

But he didn't hear her questions. He had given in to exhaustion and dropped off into a foggy sleep. She tried to keep him dry by huddling close to him, and finally she stretched out beneath the blanket with him. He murmured and put his arms around her and they tried to keep warm together. The rain was cool, the mountain air still colder, and the blanket soon became uncomfortably damp from the dripping branches above.

Shawn stirred in her arms and his eyes opened.

"Angela—"

"Feel better now?"

He sat up, looked at his swollen foot, and put his hand over his painful knee.

"As soon as the storm lets up, I'll try and find a way out."

"You can't walk!"

"I'll do my damnedest," he said. "Are you all right?"

"A little woozy in the head. It's getting better."

"Let's have some of that coffee. Maybe we can find some dry stuff and start a little fire. We'll stay put tonight and try to get help in the morning. It's going to get dark early."

"Thank goodness we have this Thermos."

"Better ration it out a little at a time," he said.

She met his eyes and read the message there loud and clear. "We're going to be lost for days, aren't we?"

"I just want to prepare you for the worst. We're down in a dense forest. I don't know who might have heard our distress call or if they got a fix on us, but I'm hoping they did. We could be close to a road. Who knows—it may only be a short hike to civilization."

She poured some of the coffee, just a few swallows apiece, but nothing had ever tasted so good. Then when that was gone, she set about searching for some dry leaves. By turning over logs and looking to the protected side of the pine trees, she found a few handfuls. Huddling around the pathetic little heap, Shawn put his lighter to it and with careful coaxing, they fanned a tiny flame. She fed it small twigs and between them kept the comforting little blaze going.

It was apparent after a couple of hours that the rain had set in for the rest of the day and probably into the night.

"Better get set for the night while it's still light," Shawn said. "If we stretch the blanket up against the wind, we'll be more comfortable and if we can keep the fire going— we still have food and coffee—tomorrow, after the sun's out, we'll find our way out."

She did what she could with the blanket. Shawn tried to help her, but the moment he was on his feet he was in such excruciating pain that he had to sit down again.

"I wasn't a girl scout for nothing, you know," she said, trying to cheer him up. "I'll handle this."

"It's a good thing. I always knew you were quite a girl, Angela."

"I have some aspirins in my purse," she said. "They might help the pain."

"I'll take a couple," he said.

He washed them down with more of the coffee, but the aspirin box held only three more tablets. She tried not to show him how badly frightened she was. How was she going to get a big, injured man out of these woods?

She finished with the makeshift shelter and went to collect more pine cones and some small branches. Inside the blanket tent the blaze took away the edges of despair.

"The rain has set in for the night," he said with a sigh.

"It would seem so."

"You're unexpectedly calm," he said with a wry grin. "I'd go down in a plane with you any old day."

"I'll never get in another plane," she said firmly.

"Sure you will. Tomorrow, when you fly on to Gatlinburg. So will I when I continue to Chicago."

"You'll never get to Chicago, not with that foot and that knee."

"Yes, I will. It will be better by morning."

Darkness was falling and Angela shivered. She wondered if there were bears around but Shawn shook his head.

"Doubtful."

"I know there are bears in these hills!"

"Honey, our luck couldn't be that rotten," he said lightly, hoping to ease her fears. "Come, sit down here with me. We'll pretend we're out on some kind of wild fling."

"Some fling," she said dryly.

She sat beside him, not only for warmth, but because she felt safer with his arms around her.

"I'll beat off the bears, honey, with my bare hands if I have to. I'll be your Davy Crockett."

"Close your eyes, Crockett. You're exhausted."

"Mmm, I am tired. The aspirins are working. I feel less pain now."

He dropped his head to her shoulder. He seemed so vulnerable, so dependent on her. All the devilment was gone, the cockiness. He was just a man, hurting, needing her, and she put her hand against his cheek, pressing his head closer to her.

"Shawn—"

"Hmm?" he asked sleepily.

"What did you say to me just before we went down?"

He half lifted his head and looked at her. "Don't remember. May Day, I suppose. May Day—"

Then he slipped away from her, his eyes closed, breathing deeply.

Perhaps she had only imagined he had shouted that he loved her. Maybe she'd only wanted to hear him say it.

Chapter XI

It was the longest night of Angela's life. The rain fell steadily, soaking everything around them. The tent dripped, the fire sputtered and struggled for life. Shawn slept fitfully, but the moment she tried to move away from him, he would clutch at her in his sleep and murmur to her.

"Don't leave me," he said.

"Only for a minute, Shawn."

He always gave her up reluctantly. Her supply of fuel for the fire wasn't going to last through the night. She went out into the driving rain to find more, but everything was wet and she didn't want to go far from the tent. The pine cones she found would have to do. Perhaps they could dry by the fire.

Shawn held out his arms to her the minute she was back and she crawled back under the blanket with him, needing the warmth of his body.

"You're shivering."

"Yes, I'm cold and soaked. I never thought I could be so cold."

"Take off your things. Maybe they'll dry if you spread them near the fire."

"No, thanks!"

"This is no time for modesty," he said.

"Sorry. I'll keep them on."

"Just want you to be as comfortable as possible."

"Believe me, I'll be more comfortable fully dressed, thank you."

He laughed softly. "I thought I really had a good chance to see you in the buff."

She flushed, the heat of her face almost welcome.

"Shut up, Shawn!"

"You have the advantage," he sighed. "I'm so darned banged up I can't even make a suitable pass at the prettiest girl in these here hills."

She managed an answering smile in the flickering light.

"Drink some of the coffee," he said.

"We'd better save it."

"A few swallows," he insisted. "There's a bottle of whiskey on the plane. Tomorrow I'll try and find it, unless it's been smashed like everything else."

The coffee was but a tease and temptation. She took only a few swallows and recapped the Thermos. Shawn pulled her close and wrapped their blanket snugly around them, but it was damp like everything else and she shivered.

"And here I thought I could heat your blood with just a look," he teased.

"Shawn, this is no time—"

"Have to think about something besides this blasted rain!" he said.

"Perhaps I should try and bandage your ankle."

"I thought of it, but let's wait until morning. Maybe some of the swelling will go down."

"How's your knee?"

"Better."

"You're lying in your teeth," she said.

With her head cradled on his shoulder, his breath brushed her face and his chin was scratchy as he leaned against her forehead.

"I hope you have a razor—"

"In my suitcase on the plane. Sorry, it's electric."

"Shawn, will they find us?"

"Shh," he said. "Shh, little darling, they'll find us. These woods aren't that big and someone may have heard us come down—we'll be okay."

He put his hand under her chin and lifted her face. Then his lips covered hers, warm and tender.

"I hope you're right," she whispered against his mouth.

"I am," he said.

He kissed her again and she moved closer. He wrapped his big body around her small one.

"Another time, another place—"

"Shh . . . Go to sleep," she said.

"Kiss me again. It makes me feel warm and good."

"It also gives you ideas," she retorted.

"I suppose if we were lost on a desert island for years, you'd still resist me."

"Probably."

"Ah, but darling, it would be such sweet surrender—"

"Go to sleep!"

With a laugh, he pressed his lips to her hair and then slowly, as she felt his arms relax around her, she knew that he had fallen asleep again. She nestled closer and tried to do the same, but her thoughts went in every direction. She wondered if anyone knew where they were. What was Aunt Franny thinking? She would have phoned Dad by now, frightened and worried. Angela took comfort in that thought. Dad would know something was wrong. He'd investigate, learn they were missing, send out a search party.

Yes, they would be found soon, probably the first thing in the morning.

It was still raining the next day. Shawn stretched beside her, wincing with a cry of pain as he tried to straighten out his knee. Then he blinked with surprise for a moment, looking at her.

"For a minute there, I forgot about the crash and where we were. It's still raining!"

"Afraid so. What would you like for breakfast? Ham or cheese?"

The sandwiches he'd brought from the Atlanta coffee shop had never looked more delicious.

"You choose," he said.

"We'll split them, half of each. And there's still coffee. I caught some rainwater in one of the paper cups—"

"I feel like a blasted idiot! I should be taking care of you, instead of you taking care of me!"

She gave him an airy shrug. "Oh, it's sort of nice to have the upper hand for a change."

They ate the food with relish. Their little fire was down to a few embers and Angela knew the first order of business was to build it up again.

"I'll try to get to the plane later and see if I can find our luggage. We could have some dry clothes—"

"It's buried in the wreckage," Shawn told her with a shake of his head. "I looked right after the crash. I couldn't pry it out. But there's no electrical storm now, so it will be safe to go aboard again. I'll go with you and see what we can do."

"You'll stay here, Shawn. Your foot isn't looking much better. Your knee is swollen, too."

"Old football injury," he said. "I wrenched it pretty badly and it seems I'm going to pay for it. How are you, darling?"

His gaze searched her face anxiously. He touched the little cut on her forehead.

"Sore?"

"Yes. I must look a sight."

His lips lifted in a roguish grin. "Honey, I think you're beautiful. I can't think of any woman I'd rather spend a night in the rain with."

She gave him an answering look. "Even Betty?"

He threw his head back and roared with laughter. "Especially Betty."

"But I heard you tell her that you loved her!"

"She's a worry wart. She'd be in a real panic if she could see me like this. Now, you, Angela, have taken it in your stride. I like that."

She finished the last of her sandwich and left the tent to search for more wood. The rain had dwindled to a drizzle, but it was still cold and uncomfortable. Once the fire had been replenished, she went back toward the plane.

It was her first good look at it and she was stunned to see how battered and crushed it was. It was a miracle they had gotten out alive!

There was a strong smell of gasoline, but she climbed aboard anyway. The luggage had been stowed in the seats behind them, but she saw that it was useless to try and get it out. Shawn was right. They would have to make do with the clothes they had on their backs. However, she could pry out her camera bag. Opening it, she saw that the lens had been crushed. She dumped out the film and extra equipment she had brought. The leather bag might serve some purpose. There was little else she could salvage but a few tools in a tool box. Shawn had already brought out everything of any use.

Shawn was trying to hobble around when she went back to their camp, but he wasn't getting along very well and she scolded him for trying.

"I suppose you're right," he admitted. "I think I'll rest another day before we try to walk out."

"I can go."

"Alone?" he asked with a scowl. "Never in a million years! I won't let you."

"But I could find help. I could at least try—"

He shook his head firmly. "No. It's best if we stay together and probably it's smart to stay here close to the plane. If they fly over and spot the wreckage, we'll signal them."

"If they fly over—if they spot us," she said with a cold shiver.

"They will," he said. "Take heart, sweetheart."

Later that morning Angela tore strips from one of the blankets and wrapped them tightly around Shawn's ankle, calling up nearly forgotten techniques learned as a scout.

"Feels better," he admits. "I'll try walking again soon. I see you brought the tool box."

"Nothing in it."

"Let me have a look."

He rummaged through it and came up with a large hunting knife. "I forgot this was in here! We can cut some pine boughs and make a softer bed than this ground."

"First cut up this old camera bag of mine into strips. We can use them to help bind up your knee and your ankle."

"Always one step ahead of me, honey," he said.

Angela studied the sky and saw that there were no breaks in the gray clouds. She couldn't see anything but trees and thicket and she couldn't hear anything but the steady drip of rain through the leaves and branches.

"We must be smack in the middle of nowhere!" she said.

Shawn nodded. "I'm afraid so. I lost all sense of direction and the wind pushed us here and there—but when I last knew, I figured we were about fifty miles from Gatlinburg."

"We may not even be in Tennessee!"

"That's possible, but I think we are."

He finished cutting the camera bag into leather strips, fastening the widest piece around his ankle for additional support, but when he tried to walk again, it was still his knee that gave him the most trouble.

"You'll only injure yourself more, Shawn," Angela said. "Don't be foolish. Let me go and see if I can find a way out."

"No!"

"Sometimes, Shawn Stevens, I could . . ."

He hobbled toward her and put his arms around her. "What, darling? What would you do?"

"I think I'd better get more firewood."

"We have enough to last all day," he said.

She tried to pull out of his arms, but he wouldn't let her. "I liked it better at night. You weren't always running away from me then."

"Honestly, Shawn, you're enough to try a woman's patience!"

"Hmm," he nodded.

Then he bent down to kiss her and she pushed him away gently, laughing.

"I wonder if there might be some wild berries. Maybe I can find some to eat."

"Just don't go out of my sight! Why don't you wait until it stops raining? You're going to catch pneumonia."

It made sense, so they crawled back into the tiny shelter of their blanket and sat down before the fire. It was painful for Shawn to lie down, but eventually he carefully stretched out his full length and put his head in her lap.

The fire snapped and crackled. The smoke drifted up through a hole in the top of the tent. The rain dripped in a hypnotic way. If she wasn't careful, Angela knew she would be lulled into a kind of dream world. It was cozy here now. Their clothes had dried from the heat of their bodies. The fire kept them warm and for the time being there were no other people in the world, no pressures, no problems.

Shawn shifted his head in her lap. "What are you thinking, darling?"

"How alone we are—away from it all."

"It's rather nice."

She laughed. "Crazy, but I was thinking the same thing. Here we are, with hardly any food, no extra clothes, miles from anywhere, you're hurt, and we're thinking what a paradise this is. Ridiculous!"

"Tell you what. Once we're out of this mess, we'll come back. We'll hike up here, packs on our back, and rough it. We'll mark this spot and come back."

"We might never find it again."

"The plane will probably rust away right here. How can we get it out? Yes, we'll find it," he said.

"Listen," she said.

"What?"

"Listen!" she said, putting her hand over his lips to silence him. "I thought I heard something."

"By heaven, it's a plane! They're looking for us, honey. Let's get out where they can see us—try to signal—wave a blanket, yell—do anything!"

But by the time she had raced to the one small clearing nearby, the plane had gone. She stood for a long time, watching the sky, waiting, hoping they'd come back, but there was nothing. She went back to where Shawn waited in the tent.

"Well?"

"They didn't see me. I don't think they even saw the plane. They just went right on over," she said with despair.

"Think, did they tip their wings?"

"No. I don't believe so."

"You're sure they didn't signal that we'd been spotted?"

"No."

He reached his arms for her. "Come back to the fire," he said. "We'll wait."

They huddled together and Angela kept listening. Now and then she went out to study the sky. Could the weather be letting up? The sky seemed lighter, the mist finer. Maybe the rain was finally moving out.

Shawn agreed with her. A little later they saw the first patch of blue sky. The rain had finally ended. Encouraged by this, they built up the fire and hung the blankets on stakes to dry. Shawn, insistent on helping, cut pine boughs to make a better bed.

"We'll stay until tomorrow morning. If the plane doesn't come back by then, we'll start walking out."

He had taken the initiative again. She knew it was pointless to argue with him. It was almost a relief that she let him take charge.

"I guess I'm not really much of a girl scout," she confessed.

"You did admirably well, darling," he said. "I'm going to try to cut some rough splints for my knee, maybe even a kind of crutch or cane. It's not going to be easy hiking out of here, even on a pair of good legs."

They spent most of the day preparing for another night in the woods and for their trek out the following morning. The skies cleared. There was the sound of a plane once, but it was some distance away. For a full ten minutes they stood craning their necks at the sky, hoping and longing, but nothing came.

By midday, their coffee was all gone. They had saved the rainwater Angela had caught and put it into the Thermos.

"We're down to the candy bars," he said. "Better save them. Can you manage to skip supper?"

"Supper? I skipped lunch, too, remember?"

"I'll make it up to you, darling. I'll buy you the biggest steak in town, once we're out of here."

"Shawn, we will get out, won't we?"

"Sure. Stop worrying."

They settled in for their second night. At least they were dry now and warm, but they kept the fire going anyway. The pine boughs made the ground less hard. Shawn spread the blanket and motioned for her to lie down.

"I'll sleep over here," she said.

His eyes flashed. "Dammit, Angela, it's going to get cold tonight. You'll sleep just like you did last night."

"No."

"All right! Have it your own way."

He gave up arguing with her and she did the best she could on a bed of pine needles, hugging her blanket around her. She was surprised to find she was so tired. The ordeal was catching up with her. When she awakened, she found herself shivering with cold. The fire had gone out. Shawn lay sprawled comfortably as she sat shivering, getting colder by the minute. She crept closer and closer to the fire.

Finally she lay down beside Shawn and his arms opened for her.

"Welcome home, darling," he said.

"You were awake all along! You let me lay there and shiver—"

"Your choice. Stop fussing and get in here with me."

She crept gratefully into his warm arms, curled against his body, and sighed.

"Cozy?" he asked.

"Very."

"Good."

Then they went to sleep, snuggled together.

When Angela awakened again, Shawn was gone. She turned over and stared up at the sky. The sun was up! Shawn came hobbling toward her.

"Time to go, darling."

"Shawn, you can't walk out of here—"

"I can try. We'll go as far as we can. We'll break camp and head east, I think. How do you feel about it?"

She looked around and nodded. "East."

"Agreed."

They kept the Thermos of water, folded the blankets and Angela rifled through her purse and took out the most valuable things. Shawn stuffed them into his pockets. Then, leaning on a kind of cane he'd fashioned with the hunting knife and a pine branch, his ankle and knee bandaged awkwardly with strips of blanket and leather, they set out.

Shawn paused for a moment and looked back at their campsite.

"We'll come back, Angela."

"Sure."

But she knew they wouldn't. Once they reached civilization and picked up the pieces of their lives again, this incident would fade. It was idiotic, but it made her feel a little sad.

It was slow going. Every step Shawn took brought new pain, but he hobbled along and when she tried to help him, he shook her away.

"Save your strength for yourself," he said.

But after an hour of painful going, she put her arm around his waist and he gave in and put his arm around her shoulder, leaning on her.

They rested often, pausing to stare up at the sky and listen. It was nearing noon, for the sun was climbing to the middle of the sky, when Angela was certain she had heard something.

"What is it, Angela?" Shawn asked.

"I thought I heard a shout. I could swear I heard my name! This must really be getting to me."

Shawn motioned for silence, cocking his head. Then he grinned. "You weren't imagining things, darling. I think we're about to be rescued. Let's give a yell, on the count of three. One, two, three—"

They screamed at the top of their lungs and then waited. An answering call came back, closer now, and Angela even imagined the sound of brush breaking under heavy boots.

They decided to wait, for Shawn was not able to go a step farther. Angela kept calling and soon their rescuers were only a few yards away.

She ran to meet them. The mountain climbers were obviously an expert team and right behind them was Michael.

"Michael!"

He looked out of his element, but he opened his arms to her with a happy laugh.

"You're safe! Thank God, you're safe."

She ran to him, for Michael represented home, her father, Emma, Casa Linda, the island of Bella Grande—everything she held dear.

His arms folded around her and he held her for a little while as tears trickled down her face.

"Easy, Angela. It's okay. You're home free now. Are you all right? Are you hurt?"

"I'm fine, but Shawn—"

The others had already found him and were administering first aid. Shawn looked up to see Angela and Michael walking toward him, their arms around each other. His eyes flickered and two spots of color came to his face.

"Hello, Field."

"Stevens," Michael nodded stiffly.

"How soon can we get home?" Angela asked.

"There's a plane waiting not far from here, and a jeep a short way down the mountain. You'll be home before you know it."

Michael pulled her closer and Angela knew how good it was to be in his strong arms, to know that soon she would be at home in her room at Casa Linda.

The rescue team fashioned a crude stretcher for Shawn and between them they carried him down to where a couple of jeeps waited. Michael and Angela went ahead and Michael was busy on the shortwave radio as they helped Shawn into the car.

"They'll relay the message," Michael said. "Your father will soon know that you've been found."

168

"And Aunt Franny?"

"He'll phone her."

Shawn looked tired and out of sorts. "Let's get this thing moving, Field, or do I have to drive myself?"

Michael gave him a cold look. "For two cents, Stevens, I would have left you there to the bears and the cougars."

"Shh!" Angela said. "Shh! Just drive, Michael. I'm so tired . . ."

The two men scarcely spoke all the way out of the hills in the jeep. The ride was rough and they bounced around. Shawn gripped his knee with his hands, his face going white.

"You should see a doctor," Michael said. "I could let you off at the first town—"

"I'll go back to Bella Grande with the rest of you," Shawn said firmly. "The company doctor can look after me there."

"Afraid something might happen you don't know about?" Michael asked with a short laugh. "How did you stand it being away all this time?"

"Just shut up, Field, before I do something about shutting your mouth permanently!"

They had reached a small Tennessee town and there, in an open field, a helicopter waited. Soon, after some trouble getting Shawn aboard, they were on their way.

Angela had sworn she would never again get into an airborne vehicle, but now it couldn't go fast enough. The sooner they reached home, the better.

Later they transferred out of the helicopter to a small private jet that belonged to the Banner Oil Company. Once aboard Shawn dropped off into a fatigued sleep and Michael poured Angela a drink from a flask.

"You need it. It must have been a terrible ordeal."

"It could have been worse."

Michael eyed her. "I just thank God you weren't hurt, Angela."

"How did you find us? You've never told me—"

"The plane spotted you. I wanted them to go back, signal you, but they were needed somewhere else. Must have been a popular time for plane crashes. Another aircraft went down too. They weren't so lucky, I hear. Both the pilot and passenger were killed."

She shuddered and the full shock of their ordeal began to set in.

"Drink up," Michael said.

"And Dad, how did he take it?" she asked.

"Like the good soldier he is," Michael said warmly. "Kelly, though, was out of her mind. And poor Emma, she wouldn't come out of her room, just stayed behind closed doors and cried."

"Shawn said we'd get out. I didn't always believe him."

Michael set his jaw. "The idiot! Why didn't he turn back when he got into the storm?"

She lifted her head and stared at him. "Where could he turn to? The storm was everywhere. We were hit by lightning. If it hadn't been for that, he would have gotten us out safely. I know he would!"

"Still defending him, I see."

She shook her dark head wearily. "I won't argue with you about him now."

Michael nodded. "Sorry."

She fell asleep before they reached home. The plane was touching its wheels to the airstrip before she realized they had reached the runways of Bella Grande. An ambulance awaited them, as well as a small cluster of people.

Shawn was taken off first and he kept looking at Angela with Michael's arm wrapped around her protectively. He gave her a dark, angry look as they took him away. Angela stepped down next and her father was there to greet her, relief in his face, his eyes brimming with tears.

"Ah, my dear Angela—"

She saw Kelly, too, rushing to meet them, breaking away from the small crowd. After greeting Angela, she went to Michael, to give him a hard hug.

"You found them. I knew you would."

"Sure, pipsqueak. No problem," Michael said with an airy shrug.

Even in her tired and stunned state, Angela saw something flash between them, a look, an expression, and her senses suddenly stood up and took notice.

170

Even José had come and Thomasita rushed to press a bouquet of flowers into her hand. José only gave her a smile, but it was as warm as a hug.

"Come see me," he said.

"Soon," she promised.

Then she was being whisked away and her father put her into his car. Behind them Michael and Kelly were driving slowly in Kelly's car and she saw in the mirror that they turned off toward the beach.

Casa Linda had never looked so good. Emma was waiting tearfully in the doorway and held her and kissed her until her heart was content. Then Angela was led to her room and told to take a bath and go to bed.

"Emma! I'm not ten years old."

"But you're tired to within an inch of your soul. Sleep. We'll have a big dinner later. Everything you like. Come now, Angela, mind your Emma."

The bath was wonderful. She luxuriated in the warm water and scrubbed off the last of the ordeal of the Tennessee mountains. Then she fell into bed, finding it unbelievably soft, and closed her eyes.

But she couldn't sleep. Strange. After only two nights, she found it hard to sleep alone, to be without Shawn's strong arms around her, his warm body there to curl up against.

Fatigue finally caught up with her. She slept, dreamed, awakened, and slept again. When she opened her eyes at last and knew that she couldn't sleep another moment longer, she dressed quickly and went out to find Emma busy in the kitchen.

"Where's Dad?" she asked.

"At the office, but he'll be here shortly. He said to be sure and keep you, not to let you go running off somewhere. He wants to talk to you."

"All right."

Her father came a few minutes later. They had a dinner that surpassed all of Emma's former efforts.

"I should get lost in the mountains more often!" Angela teased.

"Oh, don't speak of it, don't, please!" Emma said, covering her ears with her hands.

Angela's father had eaten very little. She knew that he had something important on his mind. When the last of the food was gone, he suggested they take their coffee out to the patio.

There was a cool sea breeze coming in from the Gulf. The day was ending with a brilliant sunset.

"I spoke with the doctor a while ago," he said. "Shawn's going to be all right. He'll have a stiff knee for a while and his ankle will take a few days to mend, but I think both of you were lucky."

"Very lucky."

"I may as well tell you, dear," her father said. "You know there've been changes at the office. Important changes. Its official now."

"Official?"

"About me," he said. "Shawn will be taking over my job."

"Shawn!"

"How do you feel about that?"

She swallowed a lump in her throat. "I'm not sure, Dad. How do you feel?"

He grinned at that. "I'm being transferred to our Paris office. Frankly I find the whole idea exciting. But at best, I've only a few years left to work. Two—maybe three—before I retire. I've decided to keep Casa Linda. It's been home so long."

"Oh, I'm glad! But Paris!"

"Yes. I think Shawn must have really pulled some strings to get me such a good position."

"Shawn—got you a good—"

"The best, darling," her father said. "Many people have misjudged him. I know there have been hard feelings against him. There always are when there are changes. But all in all, he will serve the island well."

"About the sabotage—"

Her father frowned. "Nothing definite, only ideas. If we could pinpoint the leader—get some real proof—well, if Shawn could clear that up, I think he'd be in solid here."

172

"Everything's changing," she said slowly. "Oh, Dad, it frightens me sometimes."

"Casa Linda won't change. It will be here whenever you want it, as often as you want. But I have an urgent phone message for you from Phillip Blazer."

She stared at him with surprise. "Phillip? I rather imagined he'd given up on me, I've taken so long in deciding—"

"Well, it must be done soon, within the next couple of days," her father explained. "I told him about the plane crash—so, he said to get in touch Sunday. Call him at home."

"The job's still there?" she asked with surprise.

Her father nodded and reached out to take her hand. "The job's there and so is he. What will you do, Angela?"

Chapter XII

They had kept Shawn in the hospital on the mainland overnight. Early the next morning Angela drove across the causeway, tossed her coins in the toll box, and made her way through the morning traffic, anticipating seeing him again.

She parked her car at the hospital and asked directions to Shawn's room. He was on the telephone, his back to her.

"It's all right, darling. I keep telling you it isn't anything serious! Just a twisted knee and a bad ankle. You know they won't keep me here for long."

Angela thought of stepping away, of waiting outside his room until he'd hung up. But then she heard him say the name Betty and her feet took root in his doorway.

"I miss you, too, dear. I can't wait to see you. I love you, Betty."

Then at last, he hung up. After a moment, he became aware of her standing in his doorway.

"Angela!"

"I see you're going to live," she said tartly. "You couldn't wait to get in touch with Betty, could you?"

He grinned at that. "So, you caught me out."

"I was going to play the good Samaritan and see if you needed anything, but I suppose Betty will be rushing here to care for you."

"Probably," he answered.

Angela flushed. She didn't know she could be so hurt or so angry. Then he raked his glance over her and beyond, searching the hallway.

"Where's Michael?"

"I wouldn't know. Working, I assume."

"He's not with you? How did that happen? After that tender scene on the Tennessee mountaintop, I rather thought—"

"I'm grateful for all you did," she said with clenched teeth, eager to have this meeting over and done. "I also thank you for being so kind to my father."

"Kind," he said, his brow arching sardonically. "I did what was right. He's been stuck on the island too long. It was time he was properly promoted. I think he was pleased with the idea of the Paris office—he'll be in full charge there, you know."

"And now I don't believe I have anything further to say to you, Shawn!"

His eyes flickered dangerously. He stirred angrily and it brought a wince of pain to his face.

"I'm sure you're dying to get back to dear Michael," he retorted.

"Good-bye, Shawn!"

With that she turned on her heel and pranced down the hall. She was still angry as she got behind the wheel of her car. She drove back to Bella Grande without getting arrested for speeding, but it was a wonder.

She was still fuming when she reached the house. Kelly's car was in the driveway and Emma called to say that her friend was waiting for her by the pool.

It was a day for confession, for eye-openers, for all kinds of surprises. The minute Angela saw Kelly she knew there was plenty in the wind. Kelly was as wound up as a top, ready to spin off into dizzy action.

"You look wonderful, Angela. After an ordeal like that—I was really worried," she said.

"Thanks, friend. So was I—at times."

They sat down in the shade of a palm tree and Emma

materialized with a tray of tinkling ice-filled glasses and a pitcher of lemonade. Kelly made small talk.

"Why don't you just spit it out, Kelly?" Angela asked at last.

Kelly gave her an uncomfortable smile. "I've never had to do this before. But you know me—I don't like keeping things from my good friends—heavens, I hope we'll still be friends—"

"Will you kindly get on with it?" Angela asked with a sigh. "I haven't got all day."

Kelly laughed. She put her glass aside and stared out to the Gulf for a little while.

"Michael wanted to do this. I wouldn't let him. I thought it was really my place—"

Angela shook her head with exasperation. Finally Kelly met her eyes and gnawed uncertainly at her lips.

"Okay, here goes," she said at last. "It's Michael—and me. I always thought—I mean I always knew—"

Angela leaned back, rather enjoying seeing her best friend squirm. Kelly was always on top of a situation, never in hot water. But she was now.

"I love him," Kelly burst out at last. "I think I have for a long time. And somehow—some way—it turns out that he cares for me, too."

"Oh!"

"What more can I say?" Kelly asked.

Then she got up, burst into unhappy tears, and ran away. Angela was stunned. For a little while, she wasn't certain how she felt. But then she had never loved Michael. Not really. He had been some kind of substitute. For Phillip.

Phillip Blazer! New York! Her old job! She must decide about all of that soon. Sunday was only two days away. Two days—maybe that was too long. Perhaps she should just pack her things and go at once.

But instead she found her way to the darkroom in the rear of the garage, turned on her red light, and locked the door. There was no film to develop. Her camera, her very best camera, was smashed in the plane crash. But there were still other prints to study, to enjoy, to perhaps enlarge. Her concentration wasn't the best and she finally put out the lights and closed the door.

The beach called. She could always sort out her thoughts there, come to decisions, find her way.

José's cottage was empty and Thomasita was nowhere about either. They must have gone fishing out in the boat. She wished she could have gone along.

It had been a long time since she had been to the little cove where she could hide from the rest of the world. Now she found herself going there again. For a long, long while she watched the sea and counted the clouds and tried to decide in which direction her life should go. She had always found peace here. Now it too was gone, like so many other good things in her life.

She heard her name shouted and looked up to find Michael down the beach, searching for her. She smiled, remembering a day not so long ago when he had come like this to tell her he was off to Chicago.

She left her hiding place with a sigh and called back. He waited for her, his tie flapping in the breeze. His eyes were narrowed and cautious as she approached him.

"You always appear out of nowhere!"

"I know," she said, linking her arm through his. "What's up?"

"Lots of things. I—I don't know how to tell you about Kelly and me—"

"No need. I'm glad. And I wish you'd tell Kelly so. She gets emotional sometimes."

Michael grinned. "Yeah, I know. Funny, we always used to fight every time we were together. Sometimes it was for fun, sometimes it had teeth in it. I suppose it was a way of denying the truth to each other. When we were fighting, we were really saying that we loved each other."

"You two will be perfect together," Angela said. "Do I get to come to the wedding?"

Michael flushed. "Not so fast! We're not going to rush into anything. I want to make sure things are going to work out first—careerwise—"

"You mean you're going to take the new job after all?"

Michael shook his head. "No. The damnedest thing has

177

happened. About half an hour ago Shawn showed up at the office on a cane, looking beat, but there, taking command."

"Oh."

"He called me in first thing. He offered me the job as his assistant. I—I'm to be his top man!"

"What!"

Michael grinned foolishly. "I don't get it, but he meant it!"

"Maybe he's fairer than you thought."

"Maybe," Michael admitted.

"And smarter, too. He knows what a good man you are, Michael."

He nodded, pleased. "Thanks, Angela. It means a lot that you think so."

"So—you and Kelly will be breezing along on top of the world!"

"It would seem so. Angela, what about you?"

They paused for a moment on the beach, the white sand hot beneath their feet, the sky drifting along as if everything was perfect in the world below. A sea gull dipped toward them, then swung away.

"I'll probably go back to New York, where I belong."

"We'll miss you."

"Thanks."

She reached up and put her arms around his neck and kissed him in a sisterly way.

"I have to get back now," Michael said. "Shawn will be wondering where I am."

"Don't keep the boss waiting."

She blew him a kiss and he hurried away with a wave. Angela folded her arms and stared out at the sea. Another piece had fallen into place.

Her father was at home when she returned to Casa Linda. He was busily clearing out papers in his desk in the study and he looked up at her with a smile.

"I was hoping you'd come soon. I'm on my way to Paris tomorrow."

"Tomorrow!"

"Shawn doesn't let grass grow under his feet."

178

"It would seem not! I just talked with Michael."

"Glad those two mended fences. I think they'll make a great team. What are your plans, Angela?"

"Oh, I wish people would stop asking me!" she said in a fit of temper.

Her father grinned at her and snapped his briefcase shut. "I've just had a brilliant idea. Come with me to Paris. Help me find a place to live, stay on to see the sights, and keep me company. We'd have a great time—almost like a holiday—"

"It's tempting," she said, "but, no, I don't think so."

Her father gave her a long, studious look. "It's going to be New York, isn't it?"

"You sound sorry."

"Only if you are," he said. "I rather thought that you and Shawn—ah, but I suppose this is wishful thinking. I think highly of that young man. We're good friends."

She couldn't stand to hear anything more good said about that scoundrel! Perhaps he was good at the office, knew his business, but when it came to women . . .

"Definitely interested in the *femme fatale*," he'd told her from the beginning.

It was proving to be true. Betty—dear Betty—seemed to have him wrapped around her little finger.

The island was changing. The Hawkinses had already gone. Dad would go next. There were many other people leaving, too, people she didn't know about—she supposed—with new ones coming in.

Since it was her father's last night in the house, Angela thought of inviting some friends for dinner, but he shook his head.

"They had a little party at the office earlier. No, I'd rather spend it here with you, dear."

"All right."

It seemed strange to think about Casa Linda without him, but he was excited and happy and she tried to match his mood. She was still trying the next morning when she drove him to the airstrip, where a company plane was waiting.

He turned to her, a slender, graying man with kind eyes and a tired face.

"Call me?" she said.

"As soon as I've settled in someplace permanent. Write me often, darling."

He kissed her and gave her a final hug. She watched while he boarded and waited for the plane to taxi down the runway and lift off. Soon it had disappeared from sight.

It was suddenly very quiet, with the roar of the plane subsiding. It was too quiet. The silence got on her nerves. She drove the car to the beach and left it. Then, kicking off her shoes, she went barefoot out to the hot sand. She knew where she was going.

José was home today. He sat on the porch smoking, a mug of coffee on the railing. Thomasita was nowhere to be seen, probably off playing with her friends.

"Hello," José said.

She sat down on the step near him. "Hello, José."

"Ah, you're sad because your papa has gone."

"Yes, I suppose so."

"More than that," he said wisely.

She dropped her head to José's knee and cried, letting her tears fall over the porch floor. With a gnarled, hardened hand, José stroked her black hair.

"There, *poca minina*. It will be all right."

"Will it, José? Everything's in such a damned mess."

"Why? You tell me why."

But she couldn't. She couldn't bring herself to say that she loved Shawn Stevens. What a fool that would make her.

She dried her tears on José's clean red handkerchief and accepted a glass of cold water. She drank it, but the knot in her throat wouldn't dissolve.

"You know what to do when you're unhappy," he said with a grin. "Go get your camera. Go to work."

She lifted her head and met his dark, wise eyes. She began to smile. It had been days since she'd had a camera in her hands.

"Maybe I will," she told him.

She lingered a little while longer and then went back down the beach to her car.

At Casa Linda she loaded her spare camera with film, regretting the loss of the good one in the plane crash. Perhaps later she would drive to the mainland and buy another one.

She shot film for more than an hour, aiming and clicking the shutter at random, knowing that she was acting very unprofessional but not caring. It kept her hands busy, focused her mind on work.

In the middle of the afternoon, while studying the prints of her morning's work, she saw Shawn next door. The real estate people were showing him the Hawkins property! Shawn was hobbling on a cane and his voice came to her on the wind.

"Very nice. Nice indeed. Yes, I like that," he was saying.

Angela began to shiver with anticipation. Shawn would be her neighbor if he bought the house. He would be just a few steps away. Then the glow faded. Betty would probably be sharing it with him. Blond, well-stacked Betty!

Emma told her the news at the dinner table.

"Did you notice? The sign next door is gone. The house has been sold."

"To Shawn?"

Emma nodded, smiling. "I hear so. My friend Stella told me. She knows the real estate people—it will be nice to have that nice Mr. Stevens next door."

Angela couldn't comment. To do so would surely choke her. Poor Emma was blinded by his charm. Shawn had done a great snow job on her!

Restless that evening, seeing a light burning next door, knowing that Shawn was there, Angela went to her darkroom. There had to be something she could do.

Snatching up some of the prints she had made before, she found herself staring at pictures of the oil depot tanks, the very tanks that had been sabotaged. One photo of them in particular had always interested her. She didn't know what seemed strange about it, but she decided to do a blow-up. The film was sharp. The enlargement should show exactly who was in the pickup truck working around the tanks.

It was a slow process. The first blow-up didn't reveal enough. She did two more, each one more refined and larger and suddenly she knew what she was seeing.

For a long, long time she looked at the evidence in her hands, the very evidence that Shawn needed to clear up the sabotage trouble.

It didn't take her long to make up her mind. She couldn't sit on information like this. She put the prints into a large brown envelope and walked next door.

Music was playing inside. For a moment she hesitated about seeing Shawn. Perhaps Betty had already arrived.

She knocked at the patio door and in a moment the music stopped and she heard Shawn hobbling toward her on his cane.

He stared with surprise when he saw her.

"Great! I was hoping you'd make a neighborly call."

"I want to show you something."

She whisked past him into the room. "How about a drink?" he asked.

"No!"

"Oh, it's like that, is it?"

She ignored the remark, just as she was doing her best to ignore his very presence. She longed to study his face, to see if he was in pain or if he was feeling better. She wanted to hold him in her arms and smooth his black hair and kiss his wide, warm mouth.

Instead she spilled the prints out on the nearest table and told him to look at them.

"What is it, Angela?"

"This was taken the morning you took me over the island in the plane. The scullduggery was going on right that minute. We must have given them a thrill or two when we buzzed over the tanks."

"I don't know what you're talking about," he said.

She circled the figure beside the tank.

"Look at this!"

He studied the print for a long moment and then raised his eyes with a startled look. "My God, this looks like—"

"Now, look at this. This is blown up still more."

"I'll be damned," he muttered.

There was one more picture, the most conclusive of all.

"There's a number on this man's hard hat, the man who is doing his darnedest to cause that tank to weaken and rupture." she said.

"Number two six seven seven. I have a hunch whom that belongs to. but I'm not sure," Shawn said.

He scooped up all the prints and returned them to the envelope. "May I keep these?"

"Of course."

He gave her a grin. "I always knew you were quite a girl, Angela."

She swept to her feet and out the door. "Along with Betty!"

He was laughing roguishly as she left. Well, she had done her good deed for the day. Now it was time to think about getting off the island, time to go back to Phillip and New York and pick up the pieces. She didn't know why she didn't phone him about her decision, but she decided to make him wait until Sunday. An eager Phillip could be very exciting.

The next day was to be Angela's last day on the island, so she drifted. She roamed the island as if she might never come back to it. She visited old haunts, and walked down the beach to see José. but found Thomasita instead.

"Grandpa went fishing with Harry."

"Oh, I see. Well, then, it's just you and me, Thomasita."

The little girl flashed her a smile and took her hand. "Can we build sand castles?"

"I'd like nothing better."

Thomasita was happy for her company and attention. They romped and played together and finally got down to the serious business of castle building. Angela watched the little girl and wondered if Phillip liked children. Would he want a girl like this, open, warm. and bright-eyed? They had never talked of children. Could she learn to love him? Once she had fancied herself in love with him. Surely there was some of that old spark left. They could make a life together, just as she and Thomasita were building the castle, taller and taller, stronger and stronger.

Then unexpectedly the whole thing collapsed and Thomasita looked crestfallen. Angela felt shocked, too.

"We can do it again, Angela," Thomasita said.

"I wonder."

She lingered for a while longer before she told the little girl good-bye and went back toward Casa Linda. She couldn't bear to go to her little hideaway, not just yet. But before she left Bella Grande, she would pay it a farewell visit.

She found Shawn waiting for her at the gates of the Casa Linda courtyard. He leaned on his cane in a triumphant way, his eyes gleaming.

"I thought you'd never come," he said.

"Sorry."

"I have news. Since you were instrumental in finding this breakthrough, I thought I should come personally and tell you about it."

"The photographs?"

He nodded. "The number led us to Harvey Davis, of all people. It didn't take long for him to panic, to break down and confess that he was behind all of it. He and two of his cronies have been arrested."

"Harvey!"

"He won't be dancing at the club for a while," Shawn said. "It seems he was sore because he thought he was going to be transferred. It was his way of getting even."

"Poor Harvey."

Shawn shook his head. "You'd feel sorry for anyone, I believe. Don't bleed for Harvey. He doesn't deserve it."

Shawn looked thin. There were still white lines of pain around his mouth. She wouldn't meet his eyes. Instead she stood waiting for him to go.

"I'm having a cocktail party tomorrow afternoon. A few of the company people are coming, a sort of housewarming. I'd like you and Michael to come too."

She stared at him. Apparently he hadn't heard about Michael and Kelly. It was just as well. Let him think what he pleased.

"I'm not sure I'll be able to come," she said, lifting her chin and meeting his eyes directly.

"Don't disappoint me."

His voice was firm and determined.

"I don't work for Banner Oil. You needn't think you can order me around!" she said.

"Oh, I think you'll come," he said confidently. "If for no other reason than to meet Betty."

With that he turned away, leaving her burning with anger. Betty! His dear Betty was going to be there. Well, she couldn't care less. One thing was certain; she would not attend the party.

But even then she was plotting what she would wear, how she would do her hair. She wanted to show everyone that Angela Wales couldn't care less about Banner Oil and everyone in it, Shawn especially. It would be her farewell to the company. Dad was away now. She wouldn't be coming back to Casa Linda often, perhaps only for a holiday now and then.

The party was well underway the next afternoon when Angela arrived fashionably late. She wore a white sundress that showed off her splendid tanned shoulders and the sheen of her dark hair. A tiny gold chain glittered at her throat. She was tuned for trouble, ready to turn on the charm, to flirt, dance, and kiss any man who was willing. She would show Shawn Stevens a thing or two!

As for Betty—she tried not to think about her. There was no woman alive she couldn't put down if she put her mind to it. She had learned this subtle art at Phillip's side. Phillip! He would be going crazy waiting for her to call— well Sunday wasn't over yet. He could wait another hour or so. She intended to make her visit to Shawn's house very brief. A token visit. He would quickly get the message that she came merely out of courtesy and nothing more.

The party sounded like a good one. The music was playing but people were too busy laughing and talking to listen or dance to it. Shawn was a perfect host and it was plain to see that after getting off to a very bad start, he had won over the people at Banner Oil.

Kelly broke away to come and meet her.

"Hi!"

"Well, so how goes it?" Angela asked.

"Fine. Really--if you're sure you're not angry—"

"I'm glad for you and Michael, silly goose. Now stop talking about it. Just enjoy."

"He's nothing short of wonderful, you know."

"Then what are you doing here, talking to me? He's waiting for you over there."

Michael saw Angela and lifted his glass to her with a smile. She blew him a kiss and turned away to find Shawn bearing down on her. He had tossed away his cane, but he walked with a stiff knee and a limp.

"I'm glad you could come, Angela."

"I only have a few minutes, I have an important phone call to make."

"Let me get you a drink—"

He was back in a moment, pressing the cold glass into her hand. Then he took her arm and propelled her into the crowd. There were calls from old friends, congratulations on the great job her photographs had done for them, and all in all, she had trouble discovering who in the crowd was Betty. Then suddenly, she saw her—small, blond, well stacked, carefully dressed. Her pleasant laughter drifted across the room to Angela.

Then Shawn was beside her again, leading her toward the strange woman.

"Betty—"

The woman turned to face them. She was lovely! But suddenly Angela saw that she was not as young as she had first thought. There were laugh lines around her eyes. Her makeup was flawless, but this woman was older, much older!

"Betty, I want you to meet Angela Wales," Shawn said.

"Ah, so I meet you at last!" Betty said warmly.

The woman's hand closed around Angela's icy fingers.

"Angela, this is Betty—sorry, I shouldn't call her that,"

Shawn said. "Bad habit I started when I was a kid. Mother, why didn't you ever make me stop that?"

Angela felt surprise leap through her like white fire.

"I should have, darling," Betty told Shawn. "But you were always a hardheaded boy."

"Are—are you here for a visit?" Angela managed to ask.

"Only long enough to help Shawn get started. Since you're next door, I may call on you for assistance now and then. I'm a stranger to the island—"

"But you won't be for long," Shawn said. "I'll expect you to visit often—"

"Yes, you'll enjoy Bella Grande, I'm sure," Angela said quickly.

Beside her Shawn was having a hard time holding in his laughter. Angela felt like a complete fool, a simpleton, an oaf. Her first thought was to escape.

She did so quickly. Shawn watched her go, the old devil shining in his eyes. Oh, what a sweet joke it was! She hated him for it. Hated him!

She couldn't go home. She couldn't bear the thought of four walls imprisoning her. Her head and her heart were reeling.

There was only one place on the island where she could go and hide and not be found or seen. She went there now, running down the beach until she was out of breath.

Once she reached her little haven, she sank down to the sand, protected from curious eyes. She pulled her knees up under her chin, wrapping her arms around them.

Betty was his mother! And he had said I love you, Angela, when the plane was about to crash. Oh, if only he did—if only . . .

Suddenly a shadow fell across her vision and she straightened with surprise. Shawn stood there, looking down at her.

"How did you find me here? No one ever sees me here. This is a very private place."

"I'd find you anywhere," he said quietly. "To the far ends of the earth, I'd find you. I'd find you even in the dark, Angela Wales."

He lowered himself beside her. Kneeling before her in the sand, he reached out and took her face in his hands.

"I thought you were giving a party," she said.

"No one will miss me. Betty will handle it."

"Betty—" she said with a smile. "I should never forgive you for that—"

"I see Michael and Kelly are a twosome these days."

"Yes."

"That leaves you—alone—free."

"If you're going to kiss me, I wish you wouldn't waste so much time talking."

He bent his head and his lips came down hard and quick, claiming her as they had never claimed her before.

"There's just one thing missing," he murmured.

"What?"

"You've never said you love me."

"Nor have you."

"I rather planned on doing that in the years ahead—sometime, when I get around to it."

Furiously she began beating his shoulders with her small fists and he laughed. Then his mouth was on hers again and she knew without a shadow of a doubt that he did love her, perhaps always had loved her.

"Ah, Shawn, I have to get back to the house," she sighed. "There's a phone call to make."

"It can wait," he whispered.

He pulled her back gently to the sand, his shoulders blocking out the sky, his eyes devouring her.

"You're everything I want, Angela. Tonight, I'm going to come knocking on your door—"

She smiled as she wrapped her arms around him. "Maybe I'll let you in, maybe I won't."

But could she keep from surrendering? Ah, sweet, sweet surrender!

"Why are we talking about it now?" he asked. "When we have this minute, this second—"

Then his lips were on hers again and the sky was lost, the gulls were hushed, even the surf seemed to pause for a moment. Just long enough for her to hear him say at last, "I love you, Angela. I love you!"

188

Love—the way you want it!

Candlelight Romances

MADELEINE A. POLLAND

SABRINA

Beautiful Sabrina was only 15 when her blue eyes first met the dark, dashing gaze of Gerrard Moynihan and she fell madly in love—unaware that she was already promised to the church.

As the Great War and the struggle for independence convulsed all Ireland, Sabrina also did battle. She rose from crushing defeat to shatter the iron bonds of tradition . . . to leap the convent walls and seize love—triumphant, enduring love—in a world that could never be the same.

A Dell Book $2.50   (17633-6)

At your local bookstore or use this handy coupon for ordering:

© 1981 B & W T Co.

Lighten up!
With low tar Belair

only 9 mg.

BELAIR